"*I never wanted...*"

Claire stopped, but Brad knew what she was going to say.

"You never wanted me here in the first place," he guessed wryly.

"Why can't you leave me alone to live my life the way I want to?" she demanded fiercely. "You...even Sally with that ridiculous trick to force us to catch her bouquet. As though anyone places any credence on that ridiculous superstition these days."

"What superstition?" Brad asked her curiously.

"The one that says the girl who catches the bride's bouquet will be the next to marry," Claire told him angrily. "Sally arranged it so that both her two bridesmaids and I were tricked into catching it."

Claire glowered at him furiously as she saw the way he had started to grin.

"Look, I've got to go," he said, "but I *am* coming back, and when I do...don't even bother to think about running away."

Dear Reader,

What is more natural than a bride wanting her closest friends also to find happiness in love? For Sally, this means tricking three of her wedding guests into catching her bouquet! Three women, each very different, but all with their own reasons for never wanting to marry. That is why they agree to a pact to stay single, but just how long will it take for the bouquet to begin its magic?

Penny Jordan has worked *her* magic on these three linked stories. One of Harlequin's most successful and popular authors, she has written three compelling romances—all complete stories in themselves—which follow the lives—and loves—of Claire, Poppy and Star. *Woman to Wed?* is Claire's story. She is Sally's youthful stepmother, whose calm, well-ordered world is about to be shattered forever.

THE BRIDE'S BOUQUET—three women make a pact to stay single, but one by one they fall, seduced by the power of love

Look out for:

#1889 Best Man to Wed? June 1997
#1895 Too Wise to Wed? July 1997

PENNY JORDAN

Woman to Wed?

Harlequin Books

TORONTO • NEW YORK • LONDON
AMSTERDAM • PARIS • SYDNEY • HAMBURG
STOCKHOLM • ATHENS • TOKYO • MILAN
MADRID • WARSAW • BUDAPEST • AUCKLAND

ISBN 0-373-11883-X

WOMAN TO WED?

First North American Publication 1997.

This edition published by arrangement with Harlequin Books S.A.

® and TM are trademarks of the publisher. Trademarks indicated with
® are registered in the United States Patent and Trademark Office, the
Canadian Trade Marks Office and in other countries.

Printed in U.S.A.

PROLOGUE

THERE has been a long tradition at weddings that the one to catch the bride's bouquet as she throws it will be the next to marry.

The bride emerged from the hotel bedroom, giving her skirts a final shake, turning round to check on the long, flowing satin length of her train before turning to smile lovingly into the eyes of her new husband.

Her two adult bridesmaids—her best friend and her husband's young cousin—and her stepmother had been dismissed for this, her final appearance in her wedding gown. Chris could be her attendant on this occasion, she had told them.

'Come on; we'd better go down,' he warned her. 'Otherwise everyone will be wondering what on earth we're doing.'

Laughing, they walked to the top of the stairs and then paused to stand and watch the happy crowd in the room below them. The reception was in full swing.

The bride turned to her husband and whispered emotionally, 'This has been the happiest day of my life.'

'And mine too,' Chris returned, squeezing Sally's hand and bending his head to kiss her.

Arm in arm they started to walk down the stairs, and then, somehow or other, Sally missed her footing and slipped. The small group of people clustered at the foot of the stairs waiting for them, alerted to what was happening by Sally's frightened cry, rushed forward, James, the best man, Chris's elder brother and two of the ushers going to the aid of the bride, whilst the two bridesmaids and the bride's stepmother reacted immediately and equally instinctively, quickly reaching out to protect the flowers that the bride had dropped as she'd started to fall.

As three pairs of equally feminine but very different hands reached out to grasp the bouquet, the bride, back on her feet now, smiled mischievously down at them and warned, 'That's it! There'll be three more weddings now.'

'No!'

'Never!'

'Impossible!'

Three very firm and determined female voices made the same immediate denial; three pairs of female eyes all registered an immediate and complete rejection of the bride's triumphant assertion.

Marry? Them? Never.

The three of them looked at one another and then back at the bride.

It was just a silly old superstition. It meant nothing, and besides, each of them knew that no matter what the other two chose to do she was most definitely not going to get married.

The bride was still laughing as she swept down the few remaining stairs on her husband's arm.

Her two bridesmaids had both already separately and jointly informed her that they had no intention of taking part in any silly old rituals which involved the degradation of them vying for possession of her wedding bouquet, and as for her stepmother...

A tiny frown pleated Sally's forehead. When would Claire accept that, at a mere thirty-four and widowed, she was not, as she always insisted, too mature to want to share her life with a new partner?

While Sally and Chris made sure that they spoke with every guest once the speeches were over, the two bridesmaids and Claire worked together to gather up the scattered wedding presents. Poppy, Chris's cousin, suddenly spotted Sally's wedding bouquet lying on one of the tables. Unable to help herself, she went over to it and picked it up, tears filling her eyes.

'Forget it,' Star, her fellow bridesmaid, instructed her, grimly removing the flowers from her tense grip. 'It's just a stupid superstition. It means nothing, and I for one intend to prove it by saying publicly and unequivocally here and now that I never intend to marry.'

As her eye was caught by an unopened bottle of champagne, she reached for it, opened it deftly and poured the foaming liquid into three empty glasses, challenging the other two, 'I'm willing to make a vow not to marry. What about you two?'

'I certainly have no plans to remarry,' Claire, Sally's stepmother, agreed more gently.

Tearfully Poppy nodded. 'I shan't marry now. Not now that Chris... Not now...' Fresh tears filled her eyes as she solemnly joined the other two in a pledge of solidarity.

All three of them raised their glasses, none of them aware that their conversation had been overheard...

CHAPTER ONE

CLAIRE MARSHALL gave a rueful look at the now empty, still confetti-strewn reception area of the hotel.

Was it really less than a couple of hours since her step-daughter and her new husband had run laughing down those stairs, trying to dodge the happy bombardment of rose petals?

Most of the guests had left now, just a small nucleus remaining in the hotel lounge. She had only come back in here to check that nothing had inadvertently been left behind.

It had been a lovely day, a perfect wedding, marred only by the fact that her husband, Sally's father, had not been with them.

It was over two years now since his death but she still missed him; he had been a good husband—kind, loving, protective. As she bent to touch the bouquet which Sally had so cleverly tricked the three women into catching, Claire acknowledged that the adjectives she was using to describe her husband were more those that she would use to describe a loving father.

'You should marry again,' Sally had urged her more than once recently. Sadness darkened her eyes. She had been lucky to find one loving and understanding man; she doubted that she would ever be lucky enough to find a second. And besides, she didn't really want to marry a second time—to make explanations, excuses or apologies.

She was distracted from her thoughts as both the adult bridesmaids came to join her. Poppy, the bridegroom's

8

cousin, glowered angrily at the bridal bouquet and curtly echoed Star's earlier bitter comment.

'No one pays any attention to those silly old superstitions these days anyway...'

Claire gave her a gentle smile. Sally had confided to her that it was an open secret in her new husband's family that his cousin had been hopelessly in love with him for years.

Poor girl, Claire thought compassionately. No wonder she looked so pale and strained; the whole day must have been an unbearable ordeal for her, and the bridegroom's brother hadn't made things any easier for her. She had accidentally come across the pair of them deep in the middle of a very angry quarrel earlier and she suspected now that at some point in the day Poppy had been crying.

'I never want to get married—never!' Poppy announced savagely now.

'A statement with which I fully concur,' the third member of the trio murmured calmly.

Claire turned her head to smile at her stepdaughter's closest and oldest friend. Claire could remember quite vividly how as a young teenager Star had always insisted that she never intended to marry and that her career was going to be the most important thing in her life.

'Such a shame that none of us truly appreciated Sally's gesture,' Claire commented ruefully as she picked up the bouquet and studied it.

'Careful,' Star warned her drily. 'You don't know what effect holding it could have...'

Claire laughed but she still replaced the bouquet. 'It is only a tradition,' she reminded the other two.

'Mmm...but perhaps for safety's sake we ought to do something constructive to ensure that we stick to the vow we made earlier and remain unmarried,' said Star.

'Such as what?' Poppy demanded, adding bitterly, 'Not that I shall ever change my mind...if I can't...' Tears were already filling her eyes. Angrily she blinked them away.

'Look, why don't we agree to meet, say, once every three months just to remind each other that we intend to stay husband-free? Then if one of us does start slipping we've always got the others to turn to for support,' Star suggested.

'*I* won't need any support,' Poppy declared.

But Claire, who could sense already how Sally's marriage was bound to alter the relationship they each had with her and one another, said firmly, 'I think that's a very good idea. Let's make a date to meet here three months from now. We can have lunch together...my treat.'

'Great, I'll put it in my diary,' Star confirmed.

Claire looked across at Poppy. She didn't know her as well as she did Star, who had been Sally's best friend ever since they had started senior school together, but she could sense how unhappy the younger girl was. It must have been hard for her, seeing the man she loved marrying someone else.

Sally had confessed that when she had first heard about Poppy she had been inclined to feel very wary of her but that once she had met her, and knowing how strong Chris's love was for *her*, she had simply felt desperately sad for her.

'It must be so awful loving someone who can't love you back in the same way,' Sally had said. 'Chris likes her, of course—she's his cousin—but...'

'But he *loves* you,' Claire had agreed.

Sally had come over to her and given her a quick hug. They had always got on well together from the moment John had introduced them. Sally had been a pupil at the huge comprehensive where Claire had done her teacher-training practice.

She had often wondered if one of the reasons why Sally had accepted her so lovingly and so readily as her stepmother had been that she had never known her own mother. Sally's mother, John's first wife, had died just after Sally's birth.

'Paula will always be part of my... of our lives. I shall always love her,' John had told her seriously when he had proposed to her.

She had accepted that, felt warmed by it, almost reassured... Knowing how much he had loved his first wife and still loved her made her feel... safe.

Sally had once asked innocently when Claire was going to have children of her own and when she was going to have a little brother or sister. Claire had had to turn away from her, leaving it to John to answer, to defuse the situation.

She sighed faintly now. Of course she would have liked children, if things had been different. As a girl she had always imagined that one day she would have them.

'I think we ought to be going now,' she told the two bridesmaids. 'I don't think we've left anything behind. I can't see anything, can you, Poppy?'

'No. There's nothing left,' Poppy agreed drearily. 'Not now.'

Claire gave her a quick look but said nothing. It seemed kinder not to.

'So now that the wedding is over, what do you intend to do with the rest of your life?'

'Oh, I don't plan to make any major changes,' Claire told her sister-in-law. 'I'm thinking of putting in a few more hours at the school but apart from that...'

Claire worked part-time as a volunteer at a local school for mentally and physically handicapped children. John had left her very well provided for financially but, as she had explained to his sister, Irene, when she had first started working at the school, she felt that she wanted to put something back into the community, and since she had originally trained as a teacher...

'Mmm, you wouldn't be interested in taking a lodger, I suppose?'

'A lodger?' Claire stared at her.

'Mmm...a colleague of Tim's who wants somewhere "home-like" to stay. A service flat is out of the question. He doesn't care for that kind of anonymity. He's an American and from a large family and he doesn't want to live alone.'

Irene went on to give her details of his background, before concluding, 'He's in his late thirties, not a young student, and it simply wouldn't be appropriate to put him in to just any kind of lodgings. He holds quite a high position in the company,' Irene said. 'In fact his family own it.'

'How high?' Claire asked her, alarm bells ringing.

'He's Tim's boss,' Irene told her a little stiffly.

'Ah, I see.' Claire grinned. 'He's Tim's boss and it's down to Tim to come up with somewhere suitable for him to stay, is that it? I can't see why you don't move him into your house, Irene,' Claire told her mock-innocently. 'After all, you've got the room, with Peter away at university and Louise working in Japan.'

'No, I don't think that would be a good idea. Things aren't going all that well for Tim at the moment—sales have dropped and there have been problems with delivery and installation. I keep telling Tim that he should be tougher, more assertive—' She broke off, shaking her head.

'Would you do it, Claire?' she asked with unfamiliar humility. 'Tim is getting himself in a dreadful state about the whole thing. Apparently this American, his new boss, is something of an... individual—'

'An individual...? What does that mean?' Claire asked her warily.

Irene started to frown. As Claire knew from past experience, likeable though her sister-in-law was, she was inclined to steamroller people in order to get her own way when it suited her, and Claire could tell that she wasn't particularly pleased at having been interrupted and questioned.

'I'm sure he's not an awkward character. Oh, Claire, I wouldn't ask you,' Irene pleaded, 'but Tim is feeling so vulnerable about his job at the moment. He has convinced himself that this American is coming in very much as a new broom; psychologically it will make him feel so much more confident if he feels that he's done something constructive ahead of his arrival...'

' "Something constructive"? Are you sure this man is going to *want* to be my lodger? From the sound of it, it seems to me that he's used to a far more luxurious lifestyle than I enjoy. You know how quietly I live, Irene. I've never been a keen socialiser.'

'No, maybe not, but people *like* you, Claire; they feel drawn to you—your house is always full of callers, your phone never stops ringing.'

Claire digested her comment in silence, knowing that it was an argument she could not refute.

John had often remonstrated with her about her tendency to attract people who needed a shoulder to cry on. The only time the big Edwardian house had ever really been quiet had been during those pitifully brief weeks leading up to John's death, and then only because Claire had specifically asked people not to call. She still missed him dreadfully—his support, his wise counsel, his protection.

His protection.

A tiny tremor shook her body.

'Irene, I don't think that it would be a good idea ... I—'

'Oh, Claire, please.'

As Claire looked at her sister-in-law she could see that her anxiety was genuine. She gave a small sigh.

'Very well, then,' she agreed. 'But I doubt that this man, Tim's new boss, is going to be very thrilled when he discovers—'

'Nonsense. Your house complies with all his stipulations,' Irene told her, then proceeded to tick them off on her fingers as she listed them.

'It's a proper home right in the centre of the community—well, at least in the best residential part of the town. You've got a proper guest suite—or at least you will have now that Sally's gone. He can have her old room and bathroom and he can use one of the other bedrooms as an office. After all, you have got five of them.

'There's a garden with adequate space for his car. He'll be part of a large family network—'

'What? There's only me,' Claire protested.

'No, there's not; there's Sally and Chris and all his family and us, and you've got enough friends to fill a fair-sized church hall twice over. You're a member at the sports club so you'll be able to take him there and—'

'I'll be able to take him *where*? Hang on a minute, Irene ...' Claire started to protest, but her sister-in-law wasn't listening to her any more.

She was standing up, reaching out to hug her affectionately and gratefully as she told her warmly and, Claire was sure, slightly triumphantly, 'I *knew* you'd do it... It's the perfect solution, after all. Tim will be so pleased and relieved. He was terrified that you might not agree, poor dear, especially since...'

'Especially since what?' Claire demanded suspiciously.

'Well, it's nothing really; it's just that this man is due to arrive tomorrow and of course he's going to expect Tim to have worked out his accommodation requirements. We've booked him into an hotel for the first couple of days...'

'He's arriving *tomorrow*?' Claire protested, and demanded, 'Irene, just how long have you known—?'

'I must run,' Irene interrupted her. 'I've promised Mary I'll give her a hand sorting out the cricket teas and I'm already late.

'We're picking Brad up from the airport when he arrives, and naturally we thought we ought to have him for dinner tomorrow evening. You'll join us, of course. It will be an ideal opportunity for him to meet you and for you to make arrangements to show him the house...'

'Irene...' Claire started to remonstrate, but it was too late. Her sister-in-law was already beating a strategic retreat.

'What on earth are you doing?'

Claire raised her flushed face from her kneeling position in the bathroom adjacent to the spare bedroom and put down her damp cloth.

She hadn't heard her friend and next-door neighbour Hannah come in.

'Clearing out this room ready for my new lodger,' she told Hannah breathlessly, and quickly explained to her what had happened.

'Oh, trust Irene; she really has pulled a fast one on you this time, hasn't she?' Hannah commented wryly. 'A lodger, and single too, I imagine, otherwise he would be looking for a house to rent. Mmm...that's going to cause a bit of excitement in the close... Wonder what he looks like...?'

'I don't know and I don't care,' Claire told her firmly, standing up and surveying the tiles she had just finished polishing with an abstracted frown, pushing one hand into her hair to lift its heavy weight off the nape of her neck.

Thick and naturally curly, its rich dark exuberance was the bane of her life. Sally often teased her enviously that, with her petite, small-boned frame and her small, heart-shaped face, framed by her glossy chestnut curls, she looked young enough to be her peer rather than almost a decade her senior.

'You should be being one of my bridesmaids,' Sally had teased her. 'You certainly look young enough to get away with it.'

Claire had shaken her head over such foolishness. She was, she had reminded her stepdaughter, a mature woman of thirty-four.

'A mature woman?' Sally had scoffed unrepentantly. 'You look more like a young girl. It's odd, you know,' she had added more seriously, 'but, despite the fact that you'd been married to Dad for over ten years when he died, there's still something almost...almost—well, virginal about you.'

She had given Claire a wry look as she'd spoken. 'I know it sounds crazy but it's true, there is, and I'm not the only one to think so. Chris noticed it as well...'

'You're unreal, do you know that?' Hannah told her fondly now. 'Here you are, an adult, fully functioning woman in the full power of her womanhood...without a man, and you turn round and tell me...'

As she saw the look Claire was giving her Hannah backed off, apologising.

'All right, all right... So I know how close you and John were and how much you must still miss him. It just seems such a waste, that's all. One thing does puzzle me, though; if this guy is Tim's boss, what on earth is he doing looking for lodgings? Why doesn't he—?'

'He wants to live in a family home,' Claire explained patiently, repeating what Irene had told her.

'Apparently he's used to having a large family around him. According to Irene, he and his brothers and sisters were orphaned when his parents were killed in an accident. He was just eighteen at the time and he stepped in as a surrogate parent, put himself and all of them through college, then took a job locally with the family business to keep the family together.'

'Oh, I see, and I suppose he was too busy taking care of his siblings to have time to marry and have his own family... Mmm... I wonder what he is like? He sounds...'

'Incredibly dull and worthy,' Claire supplied wryly for her.

Both of them started to giggle.

'I wasn't going to say that,' Hannah protested. 'Oh, by the way, what's all this about you and Sally's two bridesmaids making a pact to stay single?'

'What?'

Claire gave her a confused look and then realised what she meant.

'Oh, that... It wasn't so much of a pact, rather an act of feminine solidarity,' she explained ruefully.

'I felt so sorry for poor Poppy, Hannah. It's no secret how she feels about Chris. Sally was in two minds about whether or not to ask her to be her bridesmaid, not because she didn't want her, but because she was worried about the strain it would place her under. But, as she and Poppy agreed, for her not to have done so could have placed Poppy in an even more invidious position.

'And as for Star—well, you know her background; her mother has been divorced several times and is currently having an affair with a boy who's younger than Star and her father has, at the last count, nine children from four different relationships, none of whom he seems to have any real time for. It's no wonder that Star is so anti-marriage...'

'So it *isn't* true, then, that the three of you took a vow to support one another in withstanding the famous power of the bride's wedding bouquet?' Hannah teased her archly.

Claire stared at her.

'Who told you that?'

'Ah...so it *is* true... Someone—and I'm afraid I simply cannot reveal my source—happened to be walking past the door and overheard you.

'I don't know if it's true, but I have heard rumours that there are plans to run a book on the odds of the three of you being unattached by the time Sally and Chris celebrate their first anniversary.'

'Oh, there are, are there?' Claire retorted fiercely. 'Well, for your information... I shall never marry again, Hannah,' she said, more quietly and seriously. The laughter died from her friend's eyes as she listened to her. 'John was a wonderful husband and I loved him dearly.'

'You've only been widowed for two years,' Hannah reminded her gently. 'One day some man is going to walk into your life, set your heart pounding and make you realize that you're still very much a woman. Who knows? It could even be this American,' she teased wickedly.

'Never,' Claire declared firmly, and she meant it.

She had her own reasons for knowing that there could never be a second marriage or any other kind of intimate relationship for her, but that was something she could not talk about to Hannah, or to anyone else. That was something she had only been able to share with John, and was just one of the reasons why she still missed him so desperately.

John had known her as no one else, man or woman, had or ever could, especially no other man—most especially another man.

As he boarded his flight for Heathrow Brad Stevenson was frowning. He hadn't wanted to take up this appointment in Britain; in fact he had done every damn thing he could to try to get out of it, and in the end it had taken the combined appeal of the president of the company himself and the retired chairman to persuade him to change his mind.

As he had faced his two uncles across the boardroom table he had protested that he was quite happy where he was, that the last thing he wanted was to be sent across the Atlantic to sort out the problems they were having with the British-based offshoot of their air-conditioning company, which they had insisted on buying into, against his advice.

'OK,' he had said at the time, 'so right now Britain is sweltering in a heatwave and everyone wants air-conditioning. Next summer could be a different story and you'll be left with a warehouse full of unwanted conditioners and a long, long haul until the next hot spot.'

It had taken all his powers of persuasion then to get certain British organisations to agree to fit the air-conditioning systems in their business premises, and by doing so he had managed to avert the financial disaster with their British distribution outlet which he had predicted, but enough was enough. The thought of spending God alone knew how much time rescuing the ailing outlet

to get it running efficiently and profitably was enough
to make him grind his teeth in angry frustration.

How the hell had those two old guys guessed that he
had intended to take the easy way out and oh, so slowly
ease himself out of the business and out of the task of
eventually having to step into their shoes, which he could
see looming ominously ahead of him?

He was thirty-eight years old and there were things
that he wanted to do, things he *needed* to do, that did
not involve running a transatlantic company.

There was that boat out on the lake that he still had
only half built, for instance; that voyage he had been
promising himself that he would make ever since his high-
school days when he had earnestly traced the voyage of
Christopher Columbus through the Indies and the rich,
Spanish-owned lands of South America.

Yes, there were things he wanted to do, a life he wanted
to live, now that he was finally able to do so—now that
the last of his siblings had finally left home and got
settled.

'You watch; you'll be the next,' Sheri, the second
youngest of the family, had teased him. 'Now that you've
not got all of us at home to fuss over you'll be looking
around for a wife...raising a family with her, starting
the whole thing over again...'

'Never,' he had said firmly. 'I've done all the child-
raising I plan to do with you five.'

Sheri had given him a serious look. 'Has it really been
so bad?' she had asked him quietly, and then, answering
her own question, had said softly, 'Yeah, I guess at times
it must have been. Not from our point of view but from
yours. We've given you a hard time over the years but
you've always stood by all of us, supported us...loved
us... It hasn't really put you off finding someone of
your own, though, has it, Brad? Having your own kids?

'I mean, look at all of us... All of us married and all of us with kids except for Doug, and he's only just got married. My bet is, though, that he and Lucille won't want to wait very long. You've been so good to all of us; I hate to think—'

'Then don't,' Brad had advised her firmly, and after one look at him Sheri had acknowledged that there were times when, for all his great love for them, it was best not to push her eldest brother too far.

She didn't care to think what would have happened to them if Brad hadn't been there to take charge when Mom and Dad had been killed. There were six years between him and Amy, the next eldest, who had been twelve then, but no more than a year to eighteen months between Amy and the rest of them, going right down to Doug, who had been only just five. The accident had happened twenty years ago.

Brad had tried his best to get out of going to Britain to act as his uncle's right arm and troubleshooter, even resorting to what he had privately admitted was the unfairly underhanded ploy of laying down a set of criteria on how he wanted to live whilst he was in Britain, which he'd known full well would be virtually impossible to fulfil. Or, rather, which he had assumed would be virtually impossible to fulfil. He had not reckoned with the British distributor having a widowed sister-in-law who could, apparently, provide him with exactly the homely living accommodation he had specified.

Brad was grimacing to himself as he took his seat on the plane, but the stewardess still cast a dazzling and very approving smile in his direction. Unusually for a first-class passenger, he was wearing a pair of soft, well-worn denims and an immaculate white T-shirt that revealed the firm, tanned muscles of his arms—and hid what she suspected would prove to be the equally tanned and certainly equally firm muscles of his torso.

Generally speaking, she didn't care for such dark-haired and formidable-looking men; macho was all very well in its way, but she preferred something a little softer, a little more malleable. In *this* particular hunk's case, however, she was willing to make an exception, she decided enthusiastically.

It was true that those grey eyes looked as though they could hold a certain stern frostiness if required to do so, but there was no denying the sexual appeal of those thickly curling dark eyelashes or the hawkish, downright sexiness of that male profile with its warmly curved bottom lip.

'Miss, miss... we're Row F; where is that, please...?' Reluctantly she turned her attention to the middle-aged couple approaching her. Just her luck, she thought—it was a busy, fully booked flight and she doubted that she would get any spare time to flirt with their sexy solitary passenger.

Brad was aware of the stewardess's interest but chose to ignore it. He was not in the market for a relationship right now—of any kind. What he wanted more than anything else was to get this business in Britain all cleared up and functioning profitably so that he could hightail it back to the States and tell his uncles politely but firmly that there was no point in them looking to him to step into their shoes.

He wanted out. What he had in mind for his future was not another twenty-odd years worrying over the fate of the family business and its employees, but the freedom to pursue his own life and his own dreams.

What he had in mind was to leave work altogether, to finish building that boat of his, and then, who knew what...? To sail it around the world, maybe...? To do, in short, all the things he had never had the opportunity to do when he was younger, when he had been busy and too preoccupied with raising his brothers and sisters. He deserved some time for himself, didn't he?

He wondered briefly what the elderly widow would be like. Not too fussy and house-proud, he hoped. He was beginning to regret using that particular delaying tactic and he wondered how quickly he would be able to make his excuses to his landlady and explain that he had changed his mind and decided that it might be better if he rented himself an apartment. He had certainly never expected Tim Burbridge to come up so quickly with someone who so closely fitted all his criteria.

Worrying about hurting his prospective landlady's feelings by telling her that he had changed his mind should have been the last thing on his mind, he told himself as the plane started to lift into the sky.

Somewhere over the Atlantic he fell asleep. The stewardess paused to watch him, wondering enviously if there was already a woman in his life and how it must feel to wake up beside him every morning. Sighing regretfully, she moved further down the aisle.

CHAPTER TWO

CLAIRE was having a bad day. In fact, it had been a bad day from the moment she had woken up and remembered that this evening she was due to meet her prospective lodger for the first time. Irene had rung to stress to her how important it was that Tim's new boss was made to feel welcome and at home.

'I'll do my best,' Claire had promised meekly, but she had felt that Irene was going a touch too far when she'd informed her that she had borrowed from a friend with American connections a recipe book containing favourite traditional American recipes.

'There's a recipe in it for pot-roast, which, apparently, they love, and one for pecan pie and—'

Hurriedly thanking her, Claire had quickly brought the telephone conversation to an end. In the brief time which had elapsed since Irene had used strong-arm tactics to make her agree to help she had already begun to regret her decision, but, as yet, she had been unable to find the courage or the excuse to rescind it.

She liked Tim, who was a gentle, amiable man, technically brilliant in his field but slow to express himself verbally, unaggressive in his approach to others. She liked Irene as well, of course, but . . .

The small hand tugging on her arm distracted her from her private thoughts. She smiled lovingly and patiently as she waited for Paul to say something to her. He was the oldest of the children who attended the school, and whilst mentally extremely clever and quick, suffered very badly from cerebral palsy.

All the children were special in their own way but she had a particularly soft spot for Paul.

It was a lovely, warm, sunny spring day and, knowing how much they enjoyed the treat, she had taken Paul and one other child for a walk in the local park.

Everything had been all right until Janey, a Down's syndrome girl, had seen the ice-cream van parked by one of the exits from the park.

Both of them, of course, had wanted an ice cream, especially Janey, whose wide, loving smile touched Claire's heart every time she saw her, as did her loving hugs and cuddles.

Several other children and adults had already clustered around the van, waiting to be served, and Claire had had no inkling of what was to come as she'd joined them, although, as she had told herself bitterly later, she should have done. She was not, after all, completely unfamiliar with the cruelty with which people could sometimes treat those whom they perceived as different from themselves.

It had been a young woman who'd started it, quickly pulling her own child out of the way when pretty, brown-eyed Janey had tried to reach out and touch the girl's blonde ringlets.

'Keep away; don't you dare touch her,' she had screamed, her daughter now frightened and screaming too. Janey had also started to cry, but it had been the look of resigned knowingness in Paul's eyes that had hurt Claire most of all—that and the awareness that she could not protect him from that knowledge.

As the other woman had led her screaming child away she'd turned round and shouted to Claire.

'You ought to be ashamed of yourself. Kids like that should be with their own sort, not allowed to mix with normal kids.'

It had been Paul—bright, clever and pitifully physically limited Paul—who had asked her on the way back, 'What did she mean, Claire—our own sort...?'

She had wanted to cry then. But not in front of them. To have done so would have demeaned everything that they struggled so hard to achieve, everything that they were, but she would cry later in the privacy of the staff loo.

Now, as she walked Janey and Paul back through the park to their respective homes, Janey 'helping' to push Paul's chair, she hesitated when Paul asked if they could stop for a while to watch several children playing football.

Janey was starting to get tired and they still had several minutes before Paul's mother would be home from her part-time job, so they headed for a nearby bench.

A man was seated on it, watching the young footballers. A parent? Claire wondered. An odd feeling, unfamiliar and, because of that, all the more disconcerting, threw her very much off balance as she glanced at him. It wasn't, surely, those warmly tanned, hard-muscled male forearms revealed by the immaculate white T-shirt that were having such an extraordinary effect on her, was it?

Hastily she assured herself that it couldn't possibly be. Other women might be susceptible to that kind of arrant male sexuality, but she most certainly wasn't. Quite the opposite. Open male sexuality was something she invariably found distasteful, alarming...sometimes even threatening.

It certainly didn't normally have the effect of making her glance want to linger and examine...to explore...

A sudden flush of embarrassed, self-conscious heat flooded her body. What on earth had come over her? No wonder the man was frowning as he looked from the children to her and then back again to the children, watching them, studying them...his frown deepening as he started to stand up and walk away from them.

At her side Paul made a small, distressed sound, focusing Claire's thoughts and emotions on *his* feelings rather than her own, and a huge fierce wave of protective anger swamped her as she recognised the reason for Paul's pain.

Without giving herself time to think, she told Janey quietly but firmly to wait with Paul and then ran after the man, catching hold of his arm so that he stopped and turned round to look at her.

'How dare you do that?' she exploded. 'How dare you walk away from us like that...? Hurt *them* like that? They *are* human beings, you know, just like us. No, *better* than us, because they accept and love us. Have you *any* idea how much it hurts them when people do what you've just done? Have you *no* compassion...*no* understanding...?'

To Claire's horror she could feel her eyes starting to flood with tears, her anger starting to die away as quickly as it had arisen. What on earth had got into her? She had never in her whole life behaved so aggressively to anyone as she was to this man. It was simply not in her nature—or so she had always thought.

Thoroughly shaken by her own behaviour, and ashamed of her outburst, she turned to go but, to her shock, instead of letting her walk away the man reached out and took hold of her, imprisoning her shoulders with his strong grip.

Later, reflecting on the incident, her face burning with chagrined dismay and guilt, she wouldn't be able to understand or explain her own lack of reaction at being thus confined, or her own lack of fear, because she certainly didn't feel any.

Shock, yes. Outrage, yes. But fear? No.

'Let go of me,' she demanded, struggling to break free.

But he refused to comply, giving her a gentle little shake and telling her in a soft, slow American accent, 'Will you quit yelling at me for a breath, woman, and listen to me...?'

Listen to him.

'No, I will not,' Claire stormed back at him, her rage flooding back. 'Let me go!'

'Not until you've let me have my say, you little fire-brand. You've had yours and now it's my turn...'

'Let me go,' Claire insisted, glowering up at him.

He had the most amazingly warm grey eyes, thickly fringed with dark, curly lashes. Her breath caught in a small gasp, the look in his eyes somehow mesmerising her, so that when he cursed softly under his breath and lowered his head—his mouth—towards her own she simply stood there, her own lips softly parted...waiting...knowing...

Just before his lips touched hers, she thought she heard him mutter, 'Seems to me like there's only one way to silence a feisty lady like you,' but, since her attention was focused far more on what he was doing rather than what he was saying, she couldn't be too sure.

It was a long time since she had been kissed by a man as if she was a woman, Claire acknowledged—a very, very long time. In fact, she couldn't remember ever being kissed quite so...quite so...

Her heart started to hammer frantically against her ribs as the firm, warm pressure of a kiss meant to impose silence on her somehow or other became the slow and deliberate exploration of her mouth by lips that seemed to sense, to know...to understand... She felt herself starting to respond, her own lips suddenly pliant and soft.

With a small, outraged cry Claire wrenched herself away, her face burning not just with indignation and shock but with something far more intimate and far more worrying.

'Look, I'm sorry... I never meant... I didn't intend...' he started to apologise.

'You had no right,' Claire stormed, but he wouldn't let her finish, shaking his head and agreeing firmly.

'No, I didn't, and I'm sorry. I overstepped the mark... It should never have happened... It's just that you made me so damned mad, ripping up at me like that...

'I didn't walk away from you because of the kids,' he told her quietly. 'Or at least not in the way that you meant. That bench over there is pretty small—not much room for me and the three of you, and so I did what I thought was the gentlemanly thing and decided to move on to give you your own space. It's the kinda thing we do where I come from,' he told her pointedly.

Claire could feel her flush deepening. She had never felt more mortified or embarrassed in her life, and not just because she had totally misjudged his actions.

She turned to walk back to the children, who were still waiting patiently and anxiously by the bench, and as she did so she realised that the man had fallen into step beside her. As they reached Paul's wheelchair he crouched down beside him and, giving him a warm smile, told him conversationally, 'I spent a few months in one of those a good while back.'

Whilst Claire watched, Paul's small, thin face glowed with happy colour as he slowly showed his new friend all the things his chair could do.

Janey didn't miss out on the unexpected attention either, disengaging her hand from Claire's and going up to Paul's chair, flirting coyly.

It was only later, when Claire had delivered both children to their respective homes and she had time to herself to review the entire incident, that a horrid thought struck her.

That man, the American, he couldn't possibly be *Tim's* new boss and *her* prospective lodger, could he? No, of course he couldn't, she reassured herself. Tim's boss wouldn't be sitting on his own in a small park watching children, dressed in a T-shirt and a pair of faded jeans... He wouldn't, would he?

If it *had* been him—*if* it had been—she had probably solved the problem of trying to wriggle out of her agreement to offer him a temporary home. Irene would probably kill her, she decided faintly. No, not probably— Irene *would* kill her!

'You look very...er...formal. Where on earth are you going?' Hannah asked curiously, surveying the heavy calf-length black skirt that Claire was wearing, and its equally businesslike and repressive-looking tailored black jacket.

'Dinner at Irene and Tim's to meet my prospective lodger,' Claire told her.

'Help! Poor man!' Hannah exclaimed, gulping back laughter. 'One look at you in that outfit and he'll think he's moving in with a Victorian matron. Where on earth did you get that suit...?'

'I bought it for John's funeral,' Claire told her quietly, adding quickly when she saw the guilty chagrin in her friend's eyes, 'Oh, it's all right... I was in such a state at the time I just bought the first black suit I could find.'

'Yes...well...for a funeral...but why are you wearing it tonight? You'll be boiled alive in it, for one thing.'

'Irene wants me to make a good impression on Tim's new boss,' Claire explained.

'In that? You'll terrify the life out of him,' Hannah protested. 'You can't possibly wear it. What about that pretty knitted three-piece—the one with the little waistcoat? You look lovely in that...'

The oatmeal knitted outfit in question did suit her, Claire acknowledged. Sally had been with her when she had bought it and had insisted on her getting it, even though Claire herself had been inclined at first to think that it was too sexy for her.

'I don't think Irene would totally approve,' Claire told Hannah hastily.

'Irene might not but I'll bet your new lodger certainly will,' Hannah countered forthrightly. 'The honour of the close is at stake here, Claire; there is no way I can allow you to go out of here wearing that suit. No way at all...'

Claire gave a faint sigh, smiling ruefully at her friend.

'All right,' she agreed. 'I'll go and get changed...'

'Into the knit,' Hannah prompted.

'Into something,' Claire prevaricated.

'Into the *knit*,' Hannah said emphatically. 'And I shall come with you to make sure that you do.'

It was going to be easier to give in than to argue, Claire recognised, and if she didn't she was going to be late, which would really please Irene.

'Very well, then, the knit,' she agreed cravenly.

There was absolutely no logical reason at all for her to fear that *her* American—the American of the park— might be Tim's boss, Claire assured herself firmly as she parked her car in her sister-in-law's drive, behind Tim's large Volvo and the unexpectedly ordinary Ford which she assumed must belong to the American. After all, he had hardly looked as though he might be Tim's boss and an important, high-ranking executive with a successful

go-getting American company, did he? He had looked...
He had looked...

Hastily Claire dismissed the startlingly explicit and
detailed printout that her brain immediately produced
of the American's physical attributes and concentrated
instead on the probable appearance of Tim's boss. He
would in all likelihood be an American version of Tim—
middle-aged, well fed, business-suited, going slightly
bald.

A kind enough man, she was sure, she acknowledged
quickly. He must be, given the brief, potted history that
Irene had given her, but hardly the sort to wear the casual
garb of youth with such devastating sexiness—which *her*
American had, and with far more masculinity than the
vast majority of those young men who did wear it, Claire
admitted as she wove her way between the closely parked
cars and headed for the house.

Irene had obviously been waiting for her because she
was opening the door even before Claire knocked, beck-
oning her inside, telling her in a low voice that Tim and
Brad were in the garden.

'Brad, apparently, is a keen gardener, so at least that's
one thing you'll have in common,' she told Claire firmly
as she led the way through the house to the small sitting
room at the back where French windows led out onto a
sunken patio with steps up onto the lawn.

Two pairs of male legs were currently descending those
steps, both of them suit-trouser-clad. One pair—the
bulkier pair—Claire immediately recognised as be-
longing to Tim; the other, she decided in relief, obviously belonged to his boss.

The navy wool with the fine, barely discernible chalk
stripe running through it was such a reassuring contrast
to the well-washed, snug-fitting jeans that were now be-

ginning to haunt her that she almost laughed out aloud. How could her protagonist from the park possibly be...?

Claire literally felt the blood draining from her face as the two men finally stepped down onto the patio and came into full view.

She could feel the sharp, questioning look that Irene was giving her as she inadvertently drew in her breath in a short hiss of horror, but she refused to look back at her. She dared not do so.

Her face felt as though it was burning hot with chagrined embarrassment and dismay and she knew too that *he* had recognised her just as instantly as she had him, even though he gave no indication to the others—thankfully—as he extended his hand towards her and said formally, 'Mrs...?'

'Oh, good heavens, there's no need for such formality. Claire—Brad,' Irene announced, quickly introducing them.

'Tim, get everyone a drink, will you, whilst I go and check on dinner...?'

'I...I'll come with you and give you a hand,' Claire offered, desperate to escape.

But Irene wouldn't let her, shaking her head firmly and telling her pointedly, 'No, you stay and talk to Brad. We'll drive you over to see the house tomorrow,' she told their other guest. 'But in the meantime, if there are any questions you want to ask Claire...'

Claire could feel her heart starting to thump unevenly and heavily as he gave her a long, steady look. Her face, her whole body felt so suffused with colour that she was surprised that Irene hadn't commented on it.

'I understand you're a widow...' was his only comment as Tim, obedient to his wife's commands, bustled about getting them drinks.

'Yes...yes. John, my husband, died some time ago...'

'And you've lived on your own since then?'

Claire gave him a sharp look, made faintly uncomfortable by some undercurrent to his words. What was he trying to imply? Did he assume that just because...just because he had caught her momentarily off guard this afternoon with his...his unforgivably arrogant male behaviour in taking hold of her and kissing her...and just because, for the briefest possible smidgen of time, she might actually have involuntarily and inexplicably responded to him...that she was some kind of...that she...that her widowhood had been filled with a series of relationships...men...?

Indignation as well as a certain amount of self-conscious guilt coloured her face a soft, pretty pink, but when she opened her mouth to refute his subtle condemnation to her own shock she heard herself saying almost coyly, 'Well, no, as a matter of fact...until recently there was someone...'

It was left to Tim, returning with their drinks, to rescue her from the potential consequences of her own folly by picking up the tail-end of their conversation and telling Brad jovially, 'Claire's only been on her own a matter of days. Sally, her late husband's daughter, was living with her until she got married—'

'Your stepdaughter,' Brad elucidated, turning to take his drink from Tim with a brief smile that was far, far warmer than the one he had given her but nothing like as warm as the one he had bestowed on Paul and Janey in the park this afternoon, Claire registered, wondering at the same time why on earth she should feel so ridiculously forlorn and shut out somehow because she was excluded from that warmth.

Well, at least one thing was pretty sure, Claire decided fatalistically; now that he had recognised her and knew

who she was, Brad Stevenson was hardly likely to want
to stay with her.

For some reason, instead of the security and relief she
would have expected to feel at such knowledge she felt
a small and astonishingly painful stab of regret.

Regret . . . for what? Or would it be more appropriate
to ask herself for whom?

'Yes . . . yes. Sally, my stepdaughter,' she agreed,
flushing a little more pinkly under the look he was giving
her.

'Claire is the sort of person that others just naturally
gravitate towards,' Irene added, coming into the room
to announce that dinner was ready. 'She always seems
to have a house full of people. If John hadn't been so
much older than her I'm sure she would have filled their
home with children—'

'Your husband was a good deal older than you?' Brad
interjected, looking even more assessingly at Claire.

What on earth was wrong with the man? Why did he
have to make every question he asked her sound not
merely like an accusation but virtually like a denunci-
ation? Listening to him just then, she had heard quite
clearly the disapproval and the cynicism in his voice, and
she could see herself quite clearly through his eyes: the
young, calculating woman deliberately enticing a much
more financially well off and vulnerably older man into
falling for her.

The truth was that her relationship with John had been
nothing like that . . . nothing at all.

'He was older, yes,' she confirmed quietly now. Suddenly she felt very tired and drained. She was the one
who should be questioning him, not the other way round,
she told herself indignantly. How could she possibly
allow him to move into her home after what he had done?

But, no matter how hard she tried to stir up a sense of injustice as they made their way to the dining room, honesty compelled her to admit that the last thing she had experienced in his arms was her normal lack of interest in sensual intimacy between a man and a woman and that she had, disconcertingly, actually responded to him.

Brad might have broken all the rules by kissing her but, startled though she had been by his behaviour, it had been her own unfamiliar and totally unexpected response to him which had really thrown her.

After years of passively accepting that she was simply not a very sexual person it had not been a pleasant experience to discover that she was in danger of responding to a totally unknown man with the kind of sensual hunger that she had always associated with books and films and with having far more to do with fiction than reality.

She still wasn't quite sure which aspect of her own behaviour she found the least palatable—the fact that she had been so unexpectedly sensually aware of and aroused by him or the fact that her behaviour had made her question if she knew herself as well as she had always thought.

Both led to the kind of in-depth thinking about herself and her past which she found easier to avoid than to face, which was probably why, right now, she found herself not just embarrassed to have met Brad again but almost antagonistic towards him as well.

Once they were sitting down and eating, to Claire's mild irritation and embarrassment, Irene started to list enthusiastically Claire's domestic abilities for Brad's benefit.

'Claire is a wonderful cook,' she told him when he had commented on her own cooking. 'Of course, my brother, John, was an extremely fussy eater and he never really approved of the fact that Claire insisted on growing her own vegetables...'

'Oh?' Brad gave Claire a curious look. 'Most health-conscious people these days take the view that home-grown produce is the best.'

'Oh, it wasn't that he disapproved of that,' Irene explained. 'No, John simply thought that that kind of gardening wasn't really suitable for a woman. He—'

'My husband would have preferred me to hire someone to look after our vegetable plot.' Claire felt compelled to interrupt Irene and explain. 'He didn't think that sort of gardening was... He felt I should confine myself to—'

'John was a very old-fashioned man,' Tim cut in, giving Claire an affectionate, supportive smile. 'He believed that a woman's role in the garden should be confined to the picking and arranging of flowers.'

'John simply didn't want Claire overtaxing herself.' Irene bristled, quick to defend her brother.

'And besides, our mother always had someone in to do the heavy work. Of course, you know, Tim, that John always blamed you for Claire's interest in her vegetable garden. You were the one, after all, who encouraged her, going round there virtually every weekend to help her.'

Whilst Claire and Tim exchanged slightly guilty and conspiratorial looks Irene sighed and shook her head, grumbling about the amount of time that Tim gave to his precious garden.

Then Tim commented enthusiastically to Claire, 'I'm going to have another try with the asparagus, dig out a new bed, and I was thinking... That south wall of yours—there's no reason why we shouldn't try a grapevine on it. There are some new strains now that are far more hardy.'

'You prefer the domestic environment, then, do you, Claire?' Brad overrode Tim, his voice somehow unexpectedly hard-edged as he looked almost challengingly at her. 'You've never had any desire to have a career?' he asked pointedly, or so it seemed to Claire.

'Being a stepmother to Sally and John's wife was my career,' Claire told him stiffly.

'A career which is now over,' Brad said silkily. 'Haven't you been tempted, as so many modern women are, to take up the challenge of making a place for yourself in the commercial arena? After all, these days there is no such thing as a job for life. All of us have to be flexible, adaptable and to accept that sometimes, for our own good, we have to change career paths.'

Claire could see how nervous Brad's comments were making Tim. Was he simply trying to get at her, she wondered, or was he using her as a means of warning Tim of what lay ahead?

Either way there was something she intended to point out to him.

'I did train as a teacher,' she told him coolly. 'That's how I met John and—'

'John wanted Claire to be at home for Sally once they were married,' Irene intervened. 'She works part-time now on a voluntary basis at a special school for disadvantaged children...'

'I see... Such work must be very emotionally draining. I should have thought you would prefer the...tranquillity of your gardening.'

'Plants can be as quarrelsome and awkward in their way as children,' Claire told him with unusual sharpness as she watched the way he looked from Tim's face to her own. 'And besides, it isn't the children I find hard to deal with so much as the way that other people treat them...'

'No matter how well intentioned they are or how well drawn up, no amount of anti-discrimination laws can genuinely legislate against people's prejudices—what they feel gut-deep inside themselves,' Brad told her quietly, his earlier sharpness subsiding.

'No,' Claire agreed. 'They can't.'

'I realise that it may not necessarily be of any comfort to you, but there is a school of thought that suggests that we can and do choose what we will and will not be when we are reincarnated on this earth, and that such children bring with them special gifts of courage and understanding.'

Claire gave him a surprised look. In view of what had happened between them she had not expected him to want to offer her any kind of emotional comfort.

As though he had read her mind, he told her calmly and unexpectedly openly, 'I went through a very bad time when my folks were killed. I was very angry, very resentful, very bitter. We were never what you would call a religious family but out local pastor did his best to help. He told me that some people found it helped to view such tragedies as indications that they were stronger than others, that somehow they must be and that they would find strength to overcome whatever had happened to them. Or perhaps he simply judged that I would react better that way.'

Instead of lapsing into silence and so escaping from the extremely odd and disturbing sensations, both emotional and physical, that Brad was somehow arousing inside her—sensations which were not unlike the unpleasantness of pins and needles experienced when feeling finally started to return to a formerly numb limb, she recognised warily—she heroically subdued her instinct to retreat into herself and said firmly to Brad, 'I understand that one of the reasons you want to lodge in a family home is because you have a large family back at home in America...'

'Yes,' Brad agreed. 'I'm the eldest of six. They've all left home and established lives and families of their own now—all but the youngest... He got married a short while back. But it doesn't stop there. Ours is a small town by American standards, and at times it feels like I can't so much as walk down Main Street without bumping into an aunt or a cousin or some other relative.

'My father and his two brothers set up an air-conditioning plant in the town in the early fifties. Until recently both my uncles still worked in the business. One of them retired on doctor's orders last fall and the other...'

He paused, his eyes suddenly becoming shadowed, and Claire wondered what it was he was thinking to have caused that look of mingled anger and pain.

It was gone eleven o'clock when she eventually left, and when Brad stood up politely as she said her goodbyes and came towards her she suddenly discovered that instead of holding out her hand for him to shake she was virtually on the point of lifting her face to his... For what...? For him to kiss... And not decorously and socially on the cheek either, but as he had done this afternoon—on her lips, on her mouth, slowly caressing and exploring, making her feel... making her want.

Hot-faced, she took a quick step back from him and almost barged into Irene, who was watching her frowningly.

'Well, don't forget that we're bringing Brad round to see the house in the morning, will you?' Irene reminded her bossily as Claire turned to her. 'Will eleven suit you?'

'Eleven ... yes. Eleven's fine,' Claire agreed jerkily.

She couldn't understand why on earth Brad hadn't already said that he had changed his mind. This evening they had made polite conversation with one another but it must be as obvious to him as it was to her that it would be impossible for them to live under the same roof.

She found him far too...disturbing...far too...male, and underneath her hard struggle for an air of calm she could feel her nerve-ends bristling with anxiety-induced aggression.

Just sitting there this evening on the opposite side of the dinner table to him had mentally and emotionally exhausted her, although quite why he should be having such an extraordinary effect on her she didn't really know.

Be honest with yourself, she told herself firmly as she drove home; you never wanted to have him lodging with you. Irene caught you at a weak moment and now that you've actually met him...

Now that she had actually met him...what? Guiltily she realised that the traffic lights had changed colour and that the driver behind her was hooting impatiently for her to move off.

It wasn't dignified for a woman of her widowed status to experience emotions and physical sensations which more properly belonged to the early years of a woman's sexual burgeoning, although in her case her sexual burgeoning had been delayed so that she had assumed that it would never happen. *Had been* delayed—did that mean—?

Hastily she censored her thoughts.

Suddenly, she was defensively resentful of the way Brad's unwanted intrusion into her quiet, well-ordered life had brought to the surface issues, emotions and feelings that she had long, long ago thought safely buried.

It was a relief to get home, to walk into the familiar warmth and smell of her own kitchen.

John had originally bought the house on his marriage to Sally's mother, and, as he had explained to Claire, since it had always been Sally's home he felt it would be unfair to her to sell it and move somewhere else, especially since it was such a large and comfortable house situated in the most sought-after area of the town.

Claire had agreed with him—genuinely so. She herself had liked the house from the first moment she had walked into it, from that very first night when John had taken her there. It had felt right somehow—welcoming, warm, protective, reaching out to hold her in its sturdy Edwardian embrace.

She had known, of course, that there were other reasons why John didn't want to move. He had loved his first wife very, very much indeed. The house was a part of her, her home. Even now there were still photographs of her in the drawing room, and an oil painting of her hung at the bend in the stairs, revealing how very like her Sally was.

Some of the rooms were still furnished with the pieces of antique furniture she had inherited from her family.

Down the years Claire had lovingly cared for and polished them and when Sally had announced her engagement she had immediately offered them to her.

'No, thanks,' Sally had told her, wrinkling her nose. 'Just thinking of how much it would cost to insure them makes me feel ill.'

'But they *are* yours,' Claire had insisted. 'Your father left them to you. They were your mother's . . .'

'The best and most important gift my father ever gave me, the most valued asset he left, is *you*,' Sally had told her emotionally, hugging her fiercely, making them both cry.

'Until you came into my life, into this house, I can only remember how dull and dark my life was—how shadowed. When you came you brought the sunshine with you. When I hear people talking about wicked stepmothers I want to stand up and shout that it doesn't have to be that way, that there are "steps" who are genuinely loved and valued.

'Don't you dare even think of going out of my life, Claire,' she had told her stepmother fiercely. 'When I eventually have my children I want you there for them just like you were there for me. *You* will be their grandmother . . . you . . . and *I* will need you to be there for me and for them so much.

'I still wish that you and Dad had had children of your own, you know. I know that Dad always felt that it wasn't fair to me but he was wrong. *You* were the one he wasn't fair to, and I would have loved a brother or a sister or, even better, both . . .'

'Sometimes these things just aren't meant to be,' Claire had told her huskily.

She loved her stepdaughter as though she were her own child—had loved her from the moment John had introduced them. Sally had then been a solemn, too serious and mature child, who had stood out from her peers with her too big school uniform and the neat plaits which John had copied from photographs he'd had of Sally's mother at the same age.

It had been left to Claire to explain gently to him that Sally felt self-conscious and different because of them, that such a hairstyle was out of date and could tempt other children to pick on her and bully her.

Those first years of her marriage had been happy, productive years. Years when she had eagerly reached out to embrace the opportunity to put the past behind her—something she felt she had done very successfully and thoroughly.

So why had it now started to force its way past all the careful barriers she had erected to protect herself from it? And, more importantly, why was it Brad who was somehow responsible for the unwanted turbulence and disturbance of her normally calm and easily controlled emotions?

CHAPTER THREE

'SO COME on, then, tell me. What was he like...?'

'You'll be able to judge for yourself soon enough,' Claire told her neighbour placidly. 'Irene's bringing him round at eleven to look over the house.'

Hannah had called round ostensibly to show Claire a photograph of the hotel where she would be staying on holiday in Turkey, but Claire was more amused than deceived by her old friend's ploy to satisfy her curiosity.

'I'll go if you want me to,' Hannah offered, but without making any real attempt to dislodge herself from her comfortable seat at Claire's kitchen table.

In order to dispel some of her unwanted nervous energy Claire had been trying out a new biscuit recipe. The results of her work would be eaten by the children at the school, but there was a deeper purpose to her self-imposed task than merely the execution of her culinary skills.

The school, which was privately and voluntarily funded, with some council aid, took, in the main, children from backgrounds where for one reason or another there were certain social deprivations.

In many cases these sprang solely from the fact that the child's mother had to work and could not be there full-time, and one of the things Claire enjoyed doing was showing the children and teaching them when she could, the kind of simple domestic tasks which they would have learned as a matter of course in a different age.

The biscuit recipe she had been trying out this morning was of the very simplest variety and one she was sure that her children would thoroughly enjoy trying for themselves.

'Mmm...these are good,' Hannah opined as she sampled the first of the batch to be removed from the oven.

'I thought you were supposed to be on a diet,' Claire reminded her.

'Tomorrow,' Hannah muttered through a second mouthful of warm biscuit, turning her head in the direction of the kitchen door as they both heard a car pull up onto the drive.

'Oh, Hannah...were you just about to leave?' Irene demanded bossily as Claire opened the door to let her and Brad into the kitchen.

Hannah and Irene were old adversaries, probably because Irene knew that she couldn't boss the other woman about in the same way as she could Claire, Claire admitted wryly, mentally acknowledging that that was, perhaps, one of the reasons why she had not encouraged Hannah to leave. She didn't care to think of herself as being manipulative, but there were times...

'You must be Brad,' Hannah announced, ignoring Irene's suggestion to get up and go and shaking Brad's hand. 'I'm one of Claire's neighbours... Your neighbour too, I understand. You'll love living here with Claire; she'll spoil you to death,' she declared. 'She's a wonderful cook.'

'Mmm...smells like it,' Brad agreed pleasantly.

He was more casually dressed this morning, although not in the jeans and T-shirt in which she had first seen him. This time he was wearing a pair of plain, casual, neutral linen trousers with a white linen shirt and a soft knit neutral unbuttoned waistcoat. On another man such

clothes might have looked too stylish and uncomfortable but Brad wore them so easily that they
seemed; to be an intrinsic part of him.

There was something about a man who took an interest
in his appearance but at the same time managed to look
as if he didn't care if sticky little fingers touched his
clothes that was infinitely appealing, Claire recognised.
Too appealing, she warned herself hastily as she became
aware that Brad had turned his head and was watching
her watching him.

'I...er... Where would you like to start...? The
bedroom?' she suggested quickly, and then for no reason
that she could think of immediately blushed so hard and
so colourfully that she felt completely humiliated by her
ridiculous reaction.

What on earth had got into her? She was behaving
like a...like a... She didn't know what she was behaving like, only that she didn't care for it, she acknowledged as Irene frowned at her and told her firmly, 'Brad
will want to see the whole of the house, of course.

'My brother bought this house in the early days of his
first marriage,' she told Brad informatively as Claire
dutifully walked towards the kitchen door. 'It was very
run-down then and he and Paula completely renovated
it. Paula had very, very good taste and of course John
was well off enough to indulge her.

'It was her idea to use some of the spare bedroom
space to give each of the four main bedrooms its own
bathroom, wasn't it, Claire?' Without waiting for Claire
to reply she continued talking to Brad.

They were in the hallway now, *all* of them, Claire
noticed in mild exasperation as she opened the double
doors into the drawing room so that Brad could see for
himself the colour scheme that Irene was describing.

Claire could remember the first time she had walked into this room—how overawed she had felt by its pristine beauty and, at the same time, how protected and at peace. The whole room breathed serenity and beauty.

Without being conscious of what she was doing Claire frowned as she realised that the large, silver-framed photograph of John and Paula's wedding had been pushed to the rear of the display on the pretty Regency sofa table and her own much simpler wedding photograph pushed to the fore.

Sally, had done that, of course; she had had a bit of a thing about her father's insistence on giving prominence to his first wife's photographs, but Claire hadn't minded.

'Your late husband's first wife?'

Claire paused as Brad stepped past her and picked up the photograph she had just moved.

'Yes,' she agreed. 'Sally, my stepdaughter, is very like her mother... just as pretty, although John would never have it. In his eyes no one could ever measure up to Paula...'

She missed the frowning look that Brad gave her as he heard the conviction and warmth in her voice.

Didn't it bother her to know that her husband had loved her predecessor so much and, if not, why not? She was either an extraordinarily unusual woman or...

As he glanced around the beautiful, serenely immaculate room his eyes were caught by something that looked glaringly out of place—a very amateurishly stitched sampler which was framed and had pride of place on one of the walls.

Intrigued, he moved closer to study it.

'Paula's hobby was tapestry work,' Claire told him quietly. 'She stitched the cushions in here whilst she was pregnant with Sally. There were complications with her pregnancy which meant she had to rest.'

A small shadow touched her face. 'Unfortunately it wasn't enough and after Sally's birth... John lost her when Sally was less than three days old. It was the most terrible tragedy...'

So tragic, Brad thought, that her husband had never got over it, even though, eventually, he had found and married her, and even though, from all that Irene and Tim had told him, and from what he could see with his own eyes, she was very obviously the kind of woman whom it would be easy for any man to love... Too easy...

Brad's frown deepened. He didn't like the direction his thoughts were taking—and kept taking, in fact, ever since that incident in the park when, for God alone knew what mad, impulsive reason, he had seized hold of her and kissed her. Kissed her and felt her mouth soften into the kind of quivering, softly feminine response that he couldn't remember experiencing since he had left the heady days of his early teens behind...

'We were all thoroughly relieved when he married Claire,' Irene told him. 'There was a time when we were beginning to worry that John was trying to turn Sally into a carbon copy of Paula.'

'He was just trying to do his best for her,' Claire protested. 'He loved Paula so much... thought she was so perfect—'

She broke off as she saw the way that Brad was looking at her—the mingled pity and curiosity she thought were in his eyes. Pride and rejection of his unwanted compassion sparkled in her own eyes as she lifted her head and looked back at him.

Her upbringing had had its share of pain, like Sally's. Orphaned whilst she was still a toddler, she had been brought up by a maiden aunt of her father's—a retired

schoolteacher who had had very strong views on the way
that children and most especially girls should behave.

Under her tutelage Claire had developed into an in-
telligent but socially shy and uncertain girl with very little
in common with her peers.

Her great-aunt had died unexpectedly from a fatal
heart attack whilst Claire was coming to the end of her
teacher training. She had first met John a few weeks
later, just after...

Brad, who was still watching her, wondered what it was
that had suddenly made her look so haunted.

Despite the obvious tension it was causing between
them, he couldn't bring himself to regret totally what
had happened at their first meeting, but the passionately
vibrant woman she had been then seemed curiously at
odds with the woman she appeared to be now—a woman
who seemed quite content passively to accept her role as
a very poor second best to her husband's first wife.

She was such an obviously sensual and loving woman
that he couldn't imagine how she could ever have been
happy with a man who, from what he had heard about
him, could not possibly have met and satisfied her
emotional needs—or her physical ones either.

He frowned, angry with himself for the probing intimacy of his thoughts.

But he had seen for himself how warm and womanly
she was, both with the children and with Tim, her gentle
smile taking the edge off Irene's almost acerbic comments to her husband.

It was, perhaps, no wonder that Tim should choose
to spend so much of his free time helping Claire with
her gardening.

His frown deepened as he wondered if the relationship between them was as innocent as it had first seemed.

There had been nothing so far in Irene's manner towards either her husband or her sister-in-law to suggest that she suspected anything, but she was being remarkably insistent that Claire's home was the perfect place for him to lodge. Why? Because she felt that a third party living there would put a stop to any untoward intimacy between her husband and Claire?

If Claire was having a relationship with Tim, that would explain her shocked reaction to her brief response to his kiss—and the anger he had sensed in her both at dinner and again now.

He frowned again, unwilling to delve too deeply into why he should feel almost a personal sense of disappointment and loss at the thought of her being involved with another man.

What was really bugging him? The thought that his own judgement was at fault, that his first impression of her as a warm, open and very loving woman was wrong, or was it something more than mere pique at the possibility of having misjudged her?

What was Brad thinking about? Claire wondered as she saw the way he frowned. Did he, perhaps, not care for the house, or was it her he didn't like?

'If you'd like to follow me...' she told him, determined to sound businesslike and in control.

As he followed her up the stairs and along the landing Brad acknowledged that there was something about Claire that he found profoundly compelling; there was such a dramatic contrast between the warm, emotional woman who had flown at him with such fury to protect the feelings of her young charges and the cool, hostile person he was seeing now.

Claire had stopped outside one of the bedroom doors and was waiting for him to join her. Irene and Hannah had both come with them and Irene frowned as she saw which door Claire had opened.

'But that's your bedroom—yours and John's,' she protested. 'I thought you were going to give Brad Sally's bedroom.'

'This is larger and more... more suitable,' Claire told Irene quietly.

'But where will you sleep...?' Irene demanded.

'I—'

'Look, the last thing I want is to deprive you of your bedroom...' Brad began.

But Claire shook her head quickly, her face flushing slightly as she told him, 'I...I had already decided to...to move to another bedroom. This one...John's...John's and mine,' she amended quickly, 'is too... The decor is much more suitable for a man. It has an *ensuite* bathroom and there's already a desk in the dressing room. John sometimes worked in there himself... I—'

'You've moved out of your own bedroom?' Irene was persisting, apparently oblivious to Claire's lack of enthusiasm for pursuing the subject. She looked, Brad decided, rather like a guilty schoolgirl caught out in some forbidden act.

Why? Why shouldn't she change bedroom if she wished? It was, after all, her home... her house. He remembered the look in her eyes as she had talked about her late husband's love for his first wife, the woman whose "home" it had actually been.

'I was thinking of having it redecorated. It's never been my favourite room, and—'

'But it's the master bedroom,' Irene protested.

'Yes,' Claire agreed with a quiet irony in her voice which was obviously lost on Irene but which Brad picked up on. So she was passionate and quick-witted too—a dangerously alluring combination in a woman—or so he had always felt.

The room was a good size, he acknowledged as he stepped into it, with what looked like plenty of solidly built dark wood closet space and a generously proportioned, sensibly constructed bed. As he studied it Brad let out a small sigh of relief. British standard-sized double beds did not easily accommodate a man used to the luxury of an American king-size, as he had already discovered. This bed was the only one he had seen in Britain so far that came anywhere near the spacious comfort of his own at home, even if it was a little on the high side.

As he cast his eye appreciatively and approvingly over the immaculate percale bedlinen, he acknowledged that it would be hard for him to find anything to surpass the comfort that such a bed promised. From behind him he could hear Irene saying almost accusingly to Claire, 'You've changed the bedding...'

He could sense from Claire's response that Irene's comment had embarrassed her and guessed that the new bedlinen had been bought specifically for him. She really was the most extraordinarily sensitive woman, he thought as she showed him through to the well-planned bathroom with its large bath and separate shower.

The dressing room was small, but plenty large enough for the desk and chair already installed in it, and as she waited for him to rejoin her on the landing he admitted to himself that in terms of comfort and convenience it wouldn't be easy to match the facilities of this house.

From the bedroom window he could see out into the garden. Long and wide, it was split into a series of areas by a variety of cleverly intermingled structures and plantings, and a rueful smile curled his mouth as he espied the smallest of the enclosed gardens with its swing and scuffed grass.

There was an area of equally stubborn baldness on his own lawn back home. When he had threatened to have the swing removed and the area reseeded the previous fall, the whole family had been up in arms, protesting against the removal of one of their sacred childhood haunts. The house was far too large for him now, of course. He really ought to sell it...

Outside on the landing Claire could feel her face start to flush defensively as Irene reiterated, 'Claire, I thought you were going to give him Sally's old room...'

'I...I didn't think it would be very suitable. The decor is so very feminine,' Claire told her, unwilling to admit that she had not wanted her stepdaughter to return from her honeymoon to find that someone else had taken over her old bedroom.

Sensitively she wanted Sally to be able to feel that the house was still her home, that her room was still her own and that she could return to it whenever she wished. Not that she anticipated that Sally would ever do so—nor did she want her to: her place, her home now was with her new husband.

'But to move out of your own bedroom...' Irene protested.

'It isn't my room,' Claire told her. 'It was John's room—our room,' she amended hurriedly as she saw Brad walking towards them. How could she explain to Irene—to anyone—how, after John had died, instead of finding comfort in remaining in the room—the bed— that they had shared during their marriage she had found it...empty and that she much preferred the smaller, prettier, warmer guest room that she had now appropriated as her own?

It hadn't been totally unfamiliar to her, after all; there had been nights during her marriage when she had woken up and, unable to get back to sleep, afraid of waking John, had crept quietly into the solitude of the guest bedroom.

'So, Brad, what do you think?' Irene demanded with the confidence of one who already knew the answer she was going to get.

'I'm sure I shall be very comfortable here,' he declared, before turning to Claire and saying, 'We haven't had an opportunity to discuss the financial details yet, I know. Would it be OK with you if I called back later...say, this evening...to do so?'

'This evening? Oh, no, I'm afraid I can't; I'm going out.'

'You're going out?' Irene frowned. 'Where...who with?'

Claire had started to walk down the stairs, and as they reached the bottom Hannah appeared in the hall just in time to catch Irene's question and to comment, with a sly smile in Claire's direction, 'Well, it can't be with a man—not unless you're cheating already...'

Cheating? Brad frowned. Did that mean that there was someone in her life? It must be a man whom she didn't want Irene to know anything about, to judge from Claire's uncomfortable and slightly hunted expression.

'It's parents' evening at school,' she explained.

'But they can't expect you to be there,' Irene said. 'You only work on a voluntary basis.'

'No, they don't *expect* it,' Claire agreed, her voice and her manner suddenly a good deal firmer. She could be firm and indeed almost aggressive in her defence of those whom she deemed vulnerable and in need of her pro-

tection, Brad guessed—be it a child or an adult.
'However, I want to be there. I'm sorry I can't see you
tonight,' she apologised to Brad. 'Perhaps tomorrow
evening.'

The effects of his long flight were beginning to catch
up on him and he still had to go out to the warehouse
to see Tim, although he didn't intend to start any in-
depth investigations into the difficulties of the British
distribution and sales side of the business as yet.

He was already aware of how on edge Tim was in his
presence and he could guess why; the spectre of redundancy haunted them all these days. Just as it no doubt
would have haunted him were he married with a not quite
fully adult and independent family.

'You should get married,' Laura, one of his sisters,
had scolded him the previous Thanksgiving. She and the
rest of them had certainly done their best to find him a
suitable wife. He found himself wondering for a moment
what they would make of Claire and then quickly caught
himself up, warily aware of how unusual it was for him
to have such a thought.

It was her differentness that intrigued him so much,
he reassured himself—the complexity and contrast of
what he had so far witnessed of her personality.

'Wow. Now that's what I call a real man,' Hannah commented, greedily munching another purloined biscuit
when she and Claire had the kitchen to themselves once
again. 'He's not at all what I expected. I thought he'd
be all crew-cut and loud checked suit.

'He's got the teeth, though,' she added thoughtfully.
'Americans always have good, strong teeth . . . all the
better to eat you with, my dear,' she added mischievously, grinning widely when Claire gave her a suspicious

look. 'And he does look as though he'd be rather good at that sort of thing...'

'If you're suggesting what I think you're suggesting—' Claire began primly, but then gave up, shaking her head as Hannah interrupted her.

'I'm not suggesting anything. I'm simply saying that he's a very...sexy man. Perhaps there *is* something in that old myth about catching the bride's bouquet, after all,' she murmured thoughtfully.

'Hannah!' Claire warned her direfully.

'All right, all right, I know—you've taken a vow of celibacy and I shan't say another word; it just seems such a pity that it's all such a waste...'

After Hannah had gone, taking the rest of the biscuits with her, Claire walked slowly upstairs and then paused outside the door to the master bedroom, pushing it open slowly, with reluctance almost, pausing on the threshold before eventually walking inside.

This was the room she had shared with John throughout their marriage—as a bride and a young wife—but when she stood still in its centre there were no echoes of those years to ruffle its almost sterile blankness.

There was no sense, no awareness, no feeling in this room of people having lived intimately within the protection of its walls, of having laughed and cried, fought and made up, of having shared intimacies...of having loved. She had seen the way that Brad had frowned as he had studied the room and had worried anxiously that he too might have picked up on the room's lack of those intimate vibrations.

It was strange how one became accustomed to things, adapted to them, accepted them and eventually came to think of them as the norm. It took something—*someone* different to make one see things from a different perspective—to make one realise.

As she smoothed down the already smooth cover on the bed Claire realised that her hand was trembling. Her marriage...her life...her...her privacy...they belonged to her and to no one else. There was no need for her to worry that someone else—that anyone else—would ever discover them, she reassured herself firmly.

The only way he...*they* could ever do so would be if she chose to tell them, and since she was certainly not going to do that...

Brad was halfway through his meeting with Tim when he realised that his wallet was missing. Mentally reviewing the events of the day, rerunning them through his mind's eye, he pinned down its possible loss to the moment when he had leaned forward and then bent down to inspect the workings on the shower on his tour of Claire's house. Glancing at his watch, he decided that it would probably be quicker and simpler to drive straight over than to waste time telephoning to announce his arrival.

Breaking gently into Tim's long-winded description of the vagaries of the British weather and its effect on the sales of air-conditioning systems, he explained that there was an urgent task he needed to perform.

As Brad parked his car in the drive he saw that Claire's back door was slightly open in the homely way he remembered from his own childhood, and without thinking he pushed it wider and walked in.

He found Claire in the drawing room, gently dusting the face of one of the silver-framed photographs. When she saw him she put it down quickly, guiltily almost, and for some reason the defensiveness of her action angered him, making him demand brusquely as he gestured towards the photograph, 'Wasn't there ever a time when you were jealous of her, when you resented her and wished that *you* came first, instead of always having to stand in her shadow?'

Claire's flush, initially caused by a mixture of shock at the unexpected arrival and embarrassment at the way he had caught her behaving in her own home almost as though she felt that she had no real right to be there, darkened to one of outraged anger.

'In your country it might be perfectly acceptable to make personal criticisms and to ask intimate questions, to pry into people's personal thoughts and lives, but in this country it isn't,' she reprimanded him sharply. 'My marriage—'

'Your marriage!' Brad interrupted her. 'In my country we don't classify the type of relationship you seemed to have with your husband as very much of a marriage,' he told her scornfully. 'In *my* country,' he stressed, 'no woman worthy of the name would tamely accept being pushed so obviously into second place by accepting second-best—'

'My marriage was not second-best,' Claire denied furiously. 'I knew when I married John how much he loved Paula. I knew then that...'

'That what? All he wanted you for was to care for the shrine to her that he had turned this place into? And you were happy with that... you accepted that...?'

The contemptuous disbelief in his voice stung Claire into defending herself. 'You don't know the first thing about marriage.'

'Don't I?' Brad challenged her softly. 'I know as much as any other man about what it feels like to be a man. Why did you move out of your—sorry, John's—bedroom?' he asked her.

'I... After John died...I didn't...'

'You didn't what? Like sharing your bed with a ghost? Funny that, since all your married life you'd already been sharing it with the ghost of his first wife.'

Brad didn't need to hear Claire's shocked gasp or to see the anguish in her eyes to know that he had gone too far, said too much. He had realised it almost as soon as the cruel words had left his mouth but, of course, it was too late to recall them now; too late too to curse himself under his breath and to question what on earth had prompted him, driven him—*him* of *all* men, who had surely learned years ago to deal gently with other people's vulnerable emotions; you couldn't raise four sisters without doing so—to tear away another human being's defences so ruthlessly and so angrily.

Why? Why? What was it about this one particular woman that made him react so challengingly, so malely aggressively?

'I'm sorry,' he apologised quietly. 'You're right...I was out of line. It's just...' He gestured towards the photograph and told her, 'I guess it's just that I can't help thinking how I'd feel if you were one of my sisters. It can't have been easy for you...married to a man who...'

'Who what?' Claire challenged him. 'Who loved his first wife more than he loved me?' Her mouth twisted slightly as she saw the way he looked away from her. So she had embarrassed him. Well, it served him right. He was the one who had brought up the subject of her marriage, not her, and a little embarrassment was the least he deserved to suffer after what he had said to her...done to her.

'Well, I'm not one of your sisters,' she told him fiercely, 'and my relationship with John—our marriage was...' She paused, her eyes suddenly filling with tears.

'You must have loved him very much,' she heard Brad saying gruffly, whilst he wondered how and where Tim fitted into her life.

In a way what he had said was true, Claire acknowledged inwardly, only it wasn't so much John she had loved as what he had done for her. But that knowledge, those thoughts were too private to disclose to anyone, and most especially to the man now standing watching her.

'He's been dead for over two years now and yet you still keep this place like a shrine for him,' he commented. 'Why?'

Were all Americans so forthright, so...so openly curious about other people's private lives? Claire wondered in exasperation. Wasn't there anything she could say to get it through to him that his questions were too personal and unwelcome?

'It was her home,' she told him evasively, hoping that he would drop the subject and tell her why he had returned.

Instead he pounced on what she had said with all the skill and speed of a mountain cougar, repeating softly, '*Was*... Past tense; she's in the past, but so are you. This is the present and you should put the past behind you...'

Now what had he said? Brad wondered perceptively as he saw the way her face changed, her body tensing.

'The past isn't always that easy to forget,' Claire told him in a low voice. 'Even when we want to—' She stopped speaking abruptly and Brad guessed that she had said more than she had intended.

'Why did you come back?' she asked him, changing the subject. 'Have you changed your mind about wanting to stay here...?'

She didn't really want to have him lodging with her, Brad guessed, and had no doubt been pressured into it by her over-assertive sister-in-law. Why? Because Irene was anxious to protect her husband's job or because she was anxious to protect her marriage?

Under normal circumstances the situation would have been enough to have him backing off, making some excuse to let her off the hook, but he recognised that he didn't want to lose contact with her—not yet...not until...

Not until what? Not until he had pinned down what it was about her that provoked such a range of volatile and unfamiliar emotions and reactions within him. If you really need time to work that one out, you really are in a bad way, he derided himself inwardly. She intrigued him, angered him...incited him...excited him, and if the time ever came when she shared her bed with him he'd make pretty damn sure that there were no ghostly third parties there sharing it with them.

'No, I haven't changed my mind,' he told her, pausing deliberately before adding softly, 'Far from it.'

It was interesting the way she had coloured up as betrayingly and vividly as a sexually inexperienced girl.

'I...I'd like to check over the bedroom if I may,' he continued. 'Er...which door was it...?'

Claire couldn't help it; she could feel the hot colour flooding up under her skin. She was quite positive that he knew exactly which door it was—he was that kind of man—but to challenge him would be to unleash on herself all manner of emotional hazards that she doubted that she had the strength of mind to negotiate, not least the appalling, clear mental image that she had just had of Brad laughingly, lovingly, gently drawing the shadowy figure of a compliant, eager woman towards the protective shadows of an invitingly open bedroom door, the bed just visible within—the bed on which he would very shortly be making expert and intensely erotic love to the woman clinging so eagerly to him.

But that woman wasn't her... That woman could *never* be her.

As Brad saw the way she glanced towards the stairs and the shadow that crossed her face, he felt irritably angry with himself for tormenting her. It was so out of character for him—the kind of masculine behaviour he had often verbally checked in his brothers.

'It's all right,' he told Claire quietly. 'I think I can find the way after all. It's just that I suspect I may have dropped my wallet there earlier; that's why I came back...'

'Your wallet...? Oh. I...'

He had come back for his wallet... Then why pretend...? She didn't understand. Claire frowned as she watched him taking the stairs two at a time and heading straight for the master-bedroom door.

There were a lot of things about Brad that she didn't understand, she recognised uneasily as she waited for him to come back down. But what disturbed her most was the fact that she was actually acknowledging that lack of understanding, giving it a *gravitas* that it certainly did not merit.

CHAPTER FOUR

CLAIRE grimaced to herself as she emerged from the bright warmth of the school to discover that it was raining—hard.

It had been dry and fine when she had left home earlier in the evening, and with time in hand she had decided to walk to the school instead of taking her car.

She hesitated for a moment, wondering whether or not to go back inside and ring for a taxi, and then, realising that she was already wet, pulled up the collar of her jacket and started to walk quickly down the road.

Whilst she had hesitated about whether to walk home or not she had been conscious in a hazy sort of way of the car which had pulled up at the roadside, but had assumed simply that the driver was collecting someone.

Even when she heard the engine fire and saw the brilliant sweep of the headlights illuminating the roadway ahead of her, she still didn't realise what was happening. That recognition didn't come until her brain, subconsciously waiting for the car to pick up speed and go past her, warily relayed to her senses the fact that it had not done so and what potentially that could mean.

Instinctively Claire reacted to that awareness, quickening her speed, her head tucked protectively down, her body movements designed not to draw any unwanted attention to herself as she fought not to give in to the urge to stop and turn around. She could hear the car crawling along the road behind her in much the same menacing and terrifying way that panic was now beginning to crawl its way along her tense spine.

One heard about such things... read about them—men who preyed on vulnerable, unprotected women. Her mouth had started to go dry, her heart was pounding. The area of the town she was walking through was void of any private homes—just empty shops and public buildings with no other pedestrians in sight. Whilst the rest of the traffic sped past, either oblivious to or uncaring about the slow crawl of the car behind her, it continued its slow, deliberately menacing pursuit.

Not daring to risk turning round, Claire tried to walk even faster. Beneath her clothes she could feel the hot, nervous perspiration drenching her skin; her heart was beating so suffocatingly loudly that she could no longer hear the sound of the car engine.

Her body stiffened abruptly in terrified shock as she realised why. The car had stopped. She heard the sound of a car door being slammed, followed by determined male footsteps.

'Claire... Claire...'

Claire! Her pursuer knew her name.

Trembling from head to foot, Claire turned round, her eyes widening in disbelief as she recognised Brad coming towards her.

Brad... Brad had been following her. A combination of nausea and fury gripped her by the throat, rendering it impossible for her to speak or move as Brad came up to her.

'You're soaked,' she heard him saying to her. 'Come and get in the car...' He stretched out a hand, as though to guide her towards the waiting vehicle, but Claire shrank back from it, fury burning with fevered intensity in her eyes.

'What is it...? What's wrong?' she heard him demand, impatience edging up under his voice as she pushed his hand into his own now damp hair, grimacing in disgust as the heavy droplets of rain ran down the inside of his collar.

'"What's wrong?"' Claire stared at him in disbelief; her voice was cracked and harsh. 'I thought you were following me,' she told him.

She could see from his frown that he didn't understand.

'I was,' he agreed. 'I saw you coming out of the school. I was driving past on my way to the hotel...'

As he watched the way she backed off from him Brad was filled with guilty remorse. It had never occurred to him that she would mistake him for a stranger—the kind of pervert who preyed on solitary women.

'Hey, look...it's all right,' he tried to comfort her. 'I'm sorry; I—'

'You're *sorry*...?' Claire's voice was shaking as much as her body as she flung the words back at him.

'Claire!'

'No, don't touch me,' she demanded as she stepped back still further to avoid the hand that he was reaching out to her, only to be thrown heavily against him as a runner coming the other way whom she hadn't seen collided with her, knocking her so off balance that she knew that she would probably have fallen if Brad hadn't been there to prevent it.

The runner, obviously irritated by her and the fact that she had impeded his progress, muttered an ungracious curse before continuing on his way, leaving it to Brad to ask anxiously and quietly, 'Are you OK? That was some speed he was running at—quite some speed...'

'I'm fine,' Claire fibbed.

The physical shock of almost being knocked to the ground and the emotional trauma of fearing that she was being followed, stalked, by an unknown man were both taking their toll of her. Her head felt muzzy, her thought processes were slow and confused, her hip-bone ached where the runner had cannoned into her, her stomach was still churning nauseously and the trembling which had begun when Brad had first called out to her had now become an open shivering.

Add to all that the fact that she was also extremely wet and cold and 'fine' was just about as far from describing her condition as it was possible to get.

Brad obviously thought so too, because instead of accepting her polite disclaimer as his British counterpart would have done he immediately rejected it, exclaiming curtly, 'Like hell you are! You're soaking wet through and shivering fit to bust. Come on... let's get you into the car and home. What you need right now is a shower—a proper shower, good and hot and stinging, not these apologies for showers you have over here—followed by an equally hot, stinging drink... Are you OK?' he added. 'Can you walk as far as the car or would you like me to carry you?'

Would she like him to *what*?

Claire forgot for a moment that he still had both his arms around her, and her chin came shooting up proudly as she tipped her head back to look at him. Only it wasn't his eyes which her own were on a level with. It was his mouth.

Dizzily Claire stared at it, her tongue-tip hesitantly touching her own, suddenly dry lips; a swarm of confusing and unfamiliar emotions invaded her dazed senses.

The rain had soaked her hair, causing it to curl in soft ringlet tendrils around her face, making her, although she didn't know it, look closer to twenty-four than thirty-four. In the streetlight her skin had a luminous, transparent quality that made Brad want to reach out and touch it. British women had such delicate, pale skin, and

Claire, with her fine-boned frame, had an added delicacy, a fragility almost, that aroused in him emotions...

The close contact with his body was warming her own, comforting it—an unfamiliar sensation to Claire and one that she instinctively responded to, luxuriated in on a level that was somehow beyond the jurisdiction of her normal strict self-control. Without realising what she was doing she nestled closer, exhaling her breath on a soft feminine sigh.

The hammer-blows of two different consecutive shocks had left her emotionally concussed, her senses and her emotions wandering blindly through an unfamiliar landscape where Brad was the only familiar landmark. Instinctively she clung to it... to him, her eyes huge and dazed in her pale face as she continued to focus on his mouth.

His mouth... It was strange to think that she had already been kissed by it. By him. Strange and dangerous and yet at the same time somehow headily exciting, alluring...with all the dark magic of something dangerous and forbidden.

She wanted to reach out and touch it, to trace its male shape, to...

The blare of a car horn on the opposite side of the road made her jump abruptly, bringing her back to reality, to normality.

Her face on fire with self-conscious anger and embarrassment, she tried to step back from Brad, shocked and confused by what she had been thinking—feeling.

'Come on; let's get you in the car,' he told her firmly, his voice as matter-of-fact as if it was not a very unfamiliar or shocking thing for him to have a woman staring up at his mouth... as though... as though... But then, perhaps it wasn't... She knew very little about him, after all, Claire reminded herself as she gave in and allowed him to walk her gently towards his car.

'I'm sorry I gave you such a bad shock,' she heard him apologising after he had helped her into her seat.

Claire couldn't bring herself to look at him and instead busied herself trying to fasten her seat belt. Her fingers felt numb and stiff, her actions slow and clumsy.

'It's just that I was on my way back from the office and I saw you coming out of the school and— Here, let me help you with that,' he offered, and without waiting for her agreement he gently pushed her hands away, leaning across her as he reached for the recalcitrant seat belt.

His hair was still damp and she could smell the cold, fresh scent of the rain on his hair and his skin. The nape of his neck, exposed as he leaned across her, was warmly tanned, unlike her own much paler skin. The rain had made his hair start to curl slightly.

A soft smile touched her mouth. She lifted her hand and then froze, her body stiffening in horror as she realised what she had been about to do. What on earth had come over her? The very idea... The mere thought of reaching out voluntarily to touch a man's skin... his hair... to stroke her fingers slowly through those almost boyish curls, to straighten them... was so alien to her, to everything that she was, that she could hardly believe she had actually been about to do it.

It took Brad's anxious, 'What's wrong? Is it your hip? I saw how hard he knocked you when he ran into you. It's bound to be bruised...' to bring her to her senses.

Claire felt the relief flooding through her as she realised that he thought her tension came from physical pain and hadn't understood...

'It's fine... I'm fine,' she told him brusquely.

'No, you're not,' Brad corrected her gently.

He was still leaning over her, looking directly into her eyes, and her heart gave a fierce bound as she tried unsuccessfully to look into his.

'You're probably as sore as hell... You've had a pretty nasty shock...a very nasty shock, I should say,' he amended, 'if the way you reacted earlier is anything to go by. Tell me, do you—?'

'I...I just don't like being touched,' Claire blurted out, terrified of what he might be going to ask her, to force her to reveal... 'Some people just don't...'

She was willing the betraying colour not to seep up under her skin as she made herself meet his steady scrutiny and willing herself as well not to remember the way she had practically snuggled deeper into his arms such a very short time ago, praying at the same time that he wouldn't say anything about that either.

To her relief he didn't, saying only, 'No, some people don't,' before giving her seat belt a small testing tug to make sure that it was fastened and then turning away from her to secure his own and start the car.

'I'll walk you to the door,' Brad announced after he had completed the short journey to her house.

But Claire shook her head quickly, her voice slightly huskier than normal as she said, 'No, no, it's all right...'

As he hesitated she added quickly, 'It's still raining and there's no point in you getting wet again. I've got my keys here and...'

For a moment Claire thought that he was going to insist on going with her; his body tensed and hers did too, but then he seemed to change his mind, simply telling her, 'Don't forget that hot shower or that drink. I'm not sure what time I'll be through with the hotel in the morning but I'd like to bring my stuff over before lunch if that fits in with your schedule. I've got an appointment with our bankers in the afternoon and then in the evening we can talk terms.'

'Yes. Yes, morning will be fine,' Claire confirmed.

As he watched her run towards her door through the still heavy rain Brad wondered if he was doing the right thing. There was no denying that the feeling she aroused in him, his desire for her, was more than just a subliminal male impulse.

Earlier, holding her in his arms in the street, watching the way she had looked at him . . . at his mouth . . .

Come on, he warned himself; you haven't flown right the way across the Atlantic ocean to mess up your life with those kinda complications, to get hung up on a woman who may or may not be involved with another man.

And he wasn't the sort to want to indulge in some kind of casual, no commitment, no future type of sexual fling. Nor, he judged, was she. Which meant . . . which meant that he'd better put the thoughts and desires which had been running wild through his head virtually ever since he had met her way, way back in the darkest and most unreachable recesses of his mind, he told himself firmly as he saw the door close behind Claire's retreating figure.

After a brief pause he put his hire car into gear and backed out of the drive.

'No!'

The sound of her own voice uttering the sharp, high-pitched, frantic protest brought Claire abruptly awake, to sit upright in her bed, hugging her arms around her knees as she tried to control her body's frantic shivering.

Dry-eyed, she stared fiercely into the darkness, willing the nightmare to relinquish its hold on her.

It was not as though it was something she had never experienced before, even if over the years its frequency had decreased so that now it was something that occurred only when she was under some kind of stress.

No, the reason for the agitation that she was fighting so hard to banish now wasn't so much the fact that she'd had a nightmare—it was over now, after all, and she was awake—but that somehow it had developed a new plot— a new and extremely upsetting ending.

In the past it had always followed a familiar and recognisable pattern. The man... the darkened room, his hands reaching for her... his anger when she rejected him, her escape and his pursuit down narrow, dark, wet streets in which she was completely alone and unprotected, the only sounds those of her own terrified breathing and the pounding, ever closer footsteps of her pursuer.

In the past she had always managed to escape... to wake up before he caught up with her, but this time... this time...

Her teeth chattered together as her body gave a deep shudder.

This time she had not escaped; this time he had caught up with her, his hand... both his hands... reaching for her, holding her prisoner.

She had fought frantically against the horror of his remembered and loathed touch, finally managing to turn round to face him, to plead with him for mercy.

Only when she had turned round the face she had seen had not been the one she had expected. Instead it had been Brad who had looked back at her, and inexplicably, as she'd recognised him, somehow the touch that had felt so terrifying and so loathsome had become comforting and even more disturbing, actually welcome to her body.

Relief had filled her sleep-sedated body as her fear had turned to joy, and she'd actually stepped towards him, welcoming the firm warmth of his arms around her, the scent of his skin as he'd held her close, his jaw against her hair as his arms had tightened around her and his voice had soothed her.

'It's you,' she had said softly, breathlessly as she'd pressed her trembling body against his, drawing support from his proximity and strength, luxuriating almost in the closeness of him, in the knowledge that with him she was safe and protected, trembling between laughter at her foolishness in ever having been afraid and tears because of the memories that had caused that fear.

As he'd cupped her face in his hands and bent his head to kiss her she had responded eagerly to that kiss, tightening her own arms around him, opening her mouth beneath his, anticipating in her mind the sensual pleasure of feeling his naked body against her own—a pleasure which, in her dream, both her body and her mind had recognised as one with which it was already familiar. They had not been new lovers unaccustomed to one another or unaware of one another's needs; there had been a harmony between them—an acceptance, a knowledge...

He had been so tender with her, so gentle, wiping away her tears, sharing with her her emotional relief that he was there holding her and that she had nothing, after all, to fear, that with him she was safe...protected...loved...a woman at last in every sense of the word...

A woman at last. Claire bit her lip now, balling her hands into two tight fists of angry rejection. She was already a woman; she did not need a man—any man—to reinforce that fact, and most especially she did not need Brad to reinforce it.

She had no idea why on earth she had dreamed about him like that and her face burned in the darkness as she could feel the heat of desire, her dream of him affecting her still...echoing through her body...

When Sally had talked about her marrying again it had been easy for her to shake her head and say sedately that she was happy as she was.

No needs or desires had ever troubled her celibate sleep, and a comment made by another woman friend, when they had been having lunch together one day— that the young waiter serving them had a fantastic body—had left her feeling slightly shocked that her friend should have noticed and inwardly relieved that she herself had not.

Of course, there had been occasions over the years when she had felt uncomfortable with the knowledge that her own sexuality—or rather the lack of it—was so out of step with the times, but during the years of her marriage her life had been a very busy one. John had, in his own way, been a very quietly strong-willed man, and his confidence in the way their marriage worked had made it easy for her to ignore her own doubts about her lack of sexual desire.

Before now, at thirty-four and a widow, she had felt herself safe on the small plateau of security that she had thought she had found. There had, of course, been men who had shown signs of sexual interest in her, but she had gently and tactfully made it clear that she felt no corresponding interest, and the last thing she had ever expected to happen was that she should so unwontedly and inappropriately develop a personal sexual awareness of a man.

As she continued to stare into the darkness she felt as though a part of herself had suddenly betrayed her, become alien to her...and, because of that, somehow out of her control. Dangerously out of her control, she acknowledged, blushing as she fought to ignore certain memories of just how enthusiastically and passionately she had not just responded to Brad in her dream but actually initiated the sensuality between them.

Another shudder tormented her body, her skin now chilled by the cool night air, but her heartbeat was starting to return to its normal rhythm. Tiredly Claire lay down again, closing her eyes and willing herself to go back to sleep, but this time without dreaming about Brad.

Claire smiled ruefully as she reread Sally's postcard. It had arrived in the morning's post and showed an idyllic view of a soft white half-moon beach and an impossibly azure sea—'the view from the veranda of our beach-side bungalow', Sally had written.

They were honeymooning in the Seychelles and their hotel, according to Sally's ecstatic card, was every bit as wonderful as the brochure had promised.

Typically, though, as well as reassuring Claire that she was wonderfully, blissfully happy, Sally had added a cryptic postscript to her message, teasing Claire about the fact that she had helped to catch her wedding bouquet.

'Remember,' she urged her stepmother, 'you want a man you can have all to yourself, not one you've only got a share in.' A reference, Claire knew, to the fact that she had not been the only one to catch the wedding bouquet.

The arrival of Sally's card had helped distract her thoughts away from Brad and the disruption he was causing in her life. Nonetheless, when she heard a car pulling up outside her whole body tensed, and it was a relief to discover when she went to the door that her visitor was Irene.

'I'm just on my way to the supermarket and I thought I'd call to see if you needed anything,' her sister-in-law informed her as she came in. She gave a small sigh. 'Poor Tim; he hardly slept at all last night. Claire...if Brad should happen to mention anything about the company to you—'

'Oh, I'm sure he won't,' Claire interrupted her.

'Well, maybe not, but he is, after all, over here on his own and you do have a way of... Well, people do tend to confide in you...and the two of you will be spending quite a lot of time together...'

Claire stared at her.

'No, we won't,' she protested. 'We'll hardly see one another.'

'He'll be here at mealtimes...in the evening...you'll be having dinner together,' Irene pointed out. 'I mean, that was one of the reasons he wanted to live somewhere *en famille*, so to speak—because he didn't want the anonymity of dining alone in a hotel restaurant.'

Eating together... Claire swallowed nervously.

Later, as she walked across the kitchen, the American cookery book that Irene had given her caught her eye. Glaring irritably at it, she suffered an unfamiliar surge of rebellion.

If she had to feed Brad, then at least she could exercise some form of control over the situation by feeding him food of her own choice.

Determinedly she walked towards her freezer and removed the ingredients she wanted.

John had always praised her cooking. He had liked old-fashioned, simple home-made food, and over the years Claire had found ways of adapting recipes so that she was able to satisfy his taste for the food he remembered his mother making and also ensure that the meals she served were nutritious and healthy.

She had been particularly pleased with her version of his favourite beef-steak pie. That was as traditional a British dish as you could get, especially when served with her light-as-air dumplings and garden-fresh vegetables.

Pumpkin pie and pot-roast it wasn't, but it had been Brad's desire, his decision, to live '*en famille*', as Irene had put it, and part of that, as far as she was concerned, meant eating the food *she* chose to serve.

She was too busy to be aware that it was gone eleven o'clock until she happened to look and see that it was almost twelve. Frowning, she lifted her hand to her face, depositing a smudge of flour on her cheekbone. The phone rang and she tensed. Somehow—she had no idea how—she knew that it was Brad who was ringing.

Reluctantly wiping her hands on her apron, she went to lift the receiver.

As she had known it would be, her caller was Brad.

'I'm just ringing to apologise for being late,' he told her. 'Unfortunately there was a slight problem here at the warehouse. Will it be all right if I come round now, or will that be inconvenient?'

'Now will be fine,' Claire confirmed, proud of the way she managed to keep the trembling in her body out of her voice.

Reaction set in after she had replaced the receiver, though. It was gone twelve now; would he expect her to provide him with lunch? All she had been intending to have was some left-over soup and fresh fruit. And what exactly, anyway, did he mean by saying that he wanted to live as part of a family? Hopefully, and if the hours that Tim worked were anything to go by, she wasn't going to have to see too much of him, and when she did...

Tonight, when they discussed the terms of his stay with her, she would just have to make it plain that as far as she was concerned the less contact there was between them the better.

CHAPTER FIVE

IT WAS almost one o'clock when Brad finally arrived. Opening the boot of his car, he removed a couple of suitcases and carried them into the house.

'Is it OK if I take these straight up?' he asked Claire tersely.

A little taken aback by his abrupt manner, Claire nodded.

Was he, like her, having second thoughts about the wisdom of moving in with her? she wondered as she waited downstairs for him to return.

'I'm sorry I didn't make our original time,' he apologised as he came back down again. 'There was a slight problem at the office. They had a break-in last night and although no stock was stolen we lost an extremely expensive piece of computer equipment.' His frown deepened. 'It looks very much like whoever broke in knew exactly what they were going for...'

'But what about the on-site security guards?' Claire asked him. 'Surely they must—?'

'*What* security guards?' Brad queried with dry emphasis. 'It seems that for reasons of economy the security guards had been cut down from the original four to just one, and he was in another part of the site when the break-in took place. False economy, as it turned out...'

Claire winced as she heard the irritation in his voice, her mind going anxiously and immediately to Tim. She sincerely hoped that the blame for what had happened wouldn't fall onto his shoulders; technically he was not

in charge of the site which housed the office and distribution centre...

'At least no one was hurt,' was the only comment
Claire could think of to make.

'Somebody, no,' Brad agreed, 'but something, yes.'
His voice had become a few degrees colder and very
much harder as he told her, 'Ultimately our overall
profits and, through them, the feasibility of the British
side of our business are bound to be hurt by the cost of
replacing the stolen equipment—even if our insurers pay
out it will result in an increase in our premium, plus the
business lost through the loss of the equipment...'

He shook his head, his frown lifting slightly as he
added, 'However, none of this is your concern...'

'Tim is very conscientious,' Claire felt bound to point
out to him in defence of her brother-in-law, her voice
dropping huskily. 'Irene's concerned about him. We both
are. He's been working such long hours recently and the
stress—'

'You're obviously very fond of him,' Brad interrupted
her.

'Yes, very,' Claire confirmed protectively, missing the
quick, frowning glance he gave her.

Sally's postcard lay face down on the table next to
him and he read it without meaning to. *Who* was the
man in whom Claire only had a share? Was it Tim?
Claire was certainly very close to him and very protective of him.

He liked Tim well enough—he was obviously a kind-
hearted man although a little on the weak side—but the
thought of him being Claire's lover filled him with such
a surge of angry antagonism that he knew that if Tim
had actually been there...

Hey...ease back, he warned himself. You're not here
to get involved. Just because she's alone and vulnerable,

just because it sounds like her marriage wasn't much of a marriage at all... just because she makes you feel as horny as hell and when you touch her all you can think of is taking her to bed, that doesn't mean...

'I...I'm not sure exactly what arrangements you want to come to as regards meals and so on,' he heard Claire saying. 'We haven't discussed... Irene did intimate that you wanted to live somewhere *en famille*...'

'Yes. Yes, I do,' Brad agreed, struggling to suppress an alluring vision of sharing breakfast with her, of watching her move about the kitchen, her hair still damp from her shower, her face free of make-up, her body tantalisingly naked beneath her robe.

When she stood next to him he would be able to smell the clean, fresh, feminine scent of her skin, the exposed V of the valley between her breasts headily close to him— so close that if he turned his head he would be able to reach up and pull her down onto his lap, burying his face... his mouth... in that deliciously fragranced, womanly secret place.

Was he experiencing some hormonal overload which resulted in thoughts more appropriate to one's teenage years than to one's present maturity? Brad wondered grimly.

'You'll want me to prepare dinner for you in the evening?' Claire was persisting.

'Ultimately, yes,' Brad agreed, 'but initially I'll probably be working into the evening so I'll grab something to eat myself...'

He was frowning again, remembering Tim's defensiveness over the problems he was having in meeting their high standards. It was Brad's view that Tim simply wasn't assertive enough, but he didn't want to make overhasty judgements.

He had known all along that the task his uncles had forced on him wasn't going to be easy, but now... And getting involved with Claire, when she was Tim's family and when she obviously felt so strongly about him... One thing he did know, though, he recognised, was that if she and Tim were lovers then it couldn't be a very passionate relationship.

'Is that everything?' he heard Claire asking him. 'Have you anything else to bring in from the car?'

'Er...yes...as a matter of fact there is something. I'll just go and get it...'

He was only gone a few moments, returning with what looked like a very expensive balled-up cashmere sweater, which he was carrying very carefully.

'Er...we...I...we found this in the boiler room. Looks like it's been abandoned by its mother, and I...'

The cashmere bundle started to move, a surprisingly strong mewing sound emerging from it.

'It's a cat,' Claire protested.

'A kitten,' Brad corrected her, opening the cashmere to reveal its occupant. 'Not even six weeks old yet, I guess... Too young to survive on her own, anyway, that's for sure...'

'Her?' Claire questioned.

'Well, I don't know for certain, but she's so pretty I guess I thought she had to be female,' Brad confessed, both his face and his voice softening as he gently extracted the kitten from his sweater and showed her to Claire.

Her first thought was that the animal was so small that she was almost afraid to touch her; her second was that, as Brad had said, she was extraordinarily pretty—a little fluffy tabby with white socks and huge, brave eyes.

'John didn't like animals,' she heard herself saying uncertainly. 'He would never allow them in the house... He thought—'

'*He* thought.' Brad stopped her. 'But what do *you* think, Claire?'

Claire could see the anger in his eyes although she couldn't understand the cause of it.

'This was John's home,' she reminded him with quiet dignity, 'and I—'

'And you what? You were just a visitor here? But it's your home now, isn't it? Your home, but perhaps not, after all, a home—*the* home for this little one. What she needs isn't just somewhere where she's permitted as a visitor; what she needs is somewhere where she's wanted and loved...'

For some reason his words hurt her, uncovering a wound that she had not even acknowledged was there before, Claire realised.

Without being aware of what she was doing she had stretched out her hands and taken the kitten from him. The creature felt as light as thistledown but surprisingly warm, and as Claire held her she suddenly heard the most extraordinary noise. It took her several seconds to realise what it was and when she did she exclaimed, enchanted, 'She's purring!'

'She obviously likes you,' Brad told her.

'I'll have to keep her out of the drawing room,' Claire heard herself saying crooningly as she held the kitten protectively.

'She probably can't lap properly yet,' Brad was warning her. 'You'll have to feed her with an eye-dropper for a while. Cat formula will be best... We reared three of them that way. The kids found them in an old barn. Skin and bone, they were. I never thought they'd live...'

He smiled reminiscently to himself, remembering his sister Mary-Beth's determination to save them.

He had been terrified that they weren't going to survive. It had been the first time since their parents' death that she had taken an interest in anything.

Claire started to put the kitten down and immediately she wailed in protest.

As he saw the soft, loving look in Claire's eyes Brad mentally marvelled at the ability of the young of any species to ensure their own survival.

'I've never had a cat before,' Claire told him uncertainly. 'I'm not sure what—'

'It's simple,' Brad told her. 'She'll need her own bed, some food, plenty of love—oh, and a soil tray, and you'll have to have her checked over by a good vet. Didn't you ever have any pets as a child?' he questioned her curiously.

Claire shook her head.

'No...I...I was brought up by my great-aunt. My...my parents were killed when I was very young...' She saw his face and shook his head. 'It's all right... I can't even remember them—at least, not clearly. Just...' She hesitated, not wanting to remember how often as a child she had cried herself to sleep, clinging to the memory of her mother's perfume, her father's voice...

'She...she didn't approve of pets and then John...'

Brought up by a great-aunt; that explained the air of quiet attentiveness she had, that lack of modern restlessness that could be so wearying.

He wondered if she realised quite what an intriguing person she was, and then reminded himself grimly that the other man—whoever it was that she only had a part-share in—had no doubt already told her so.

Did her relationship with him predate her husband's death? Somehow he doubted it. He could, however, well imagine her falling victim to someone in the aftermath of his death, needing someone to lean on and turn to... And who better, perhaps, than a man she already knew?

Surely she knew that it was a relationship that couldn't go anywhere, that she was demeaning herself by accepting such a meagre offering—a plastic and unsatisfying imitation of what love, commitment...sex between a man and woman should really be about?

It angered him that she could have allowed herself to be dragged into such an unfulfilling relationship. Angered him and saddened him as well.

And as for the man involved, whoever he was—Tim *or* someone else—he wasn't very much of a man, in Brad's opinion, if he could take advantage of someone so obviously vulnerable. Irritably Brad caught himself up. Take advantage of her! She was an adult woman, for God's sake, and just because she looked...and he felt...

She was still crooning softly to the cat and the thought crossed his mind that it was no wonder that her late husband had wanted her as a stepmother for his daughter. There was something about the soft, tender curve of her mouth as she held that impossibly small bundle of fluff and nothing that made his own guts ache and...

Hell, he didn't have space in his life for something like this, for someone like her. He had plans...dreams...that boat to build and sail.

'You'll have to find a name for her,' he told Claire gruffly. She flushed slightly as she acknowledged his comment. The kitten felt so soft and warm, its small body throbbing with purring pleasure as she held it.

'What about dinner this evening?' she remembered as Brad headed for the door. 'Will you—?'

'Yes, if that's convenient,' he confirmed.

He had a meeting with Tim at three and some paperwork to go through, but he guessed that he could do that later here, and he wanted to phone home, check that everything was OK, he admitted to himself. The fact that his siblings were all now adult didn't do an awful lot to lessen his feelings of responsibility towards them.

He frowned as he looked down at the postcard again. Mary-Beth had been going through a bit of a difficult time with her marriage recently. She was inclined to be very hot-headed and impulsive, with very clear and uncompromising views, outwardly strong-willed but inwardly still vulnerable.

There was a girl at work who had been making a bit of a play for her husband, and although nothing had actually happened Brad knew that she felt hurt and angry at the fact that her husband had obviously been slightly flattered by the girl's attention.

Brad could see both sides of the situation. His sister had been very wrapped up in the children recently, and her husband, Abe, whilst quite obviously loving her and their children, couldn't understand what she was so angry about, especially when he had been the one to tell her about the girl's interest in him.

Claire saw his frown deepen as he continued to stare down at the kitchen table and Sally's postcard but the kitten had started to cry, distracting her.

'Sounds like she's hungry,' Brad said. 'You could try her with a few drops of milk from an eye-dropper if you've got one.

'I'll pick up some formula and the other stuff for you on my way back to the office if you like.'

Claire stared at him. John would never have offered to do anything like that. He had been a little old-fashioned in that way, preferring to keep what he saw as their roles very clearly separate.

He had been the man of the house, the breadwinner, and financially he had made sure that Claire never had anything to worry about.

It would never have occurred to him, though, to offer to do any shopping for her and she knew that he would have been horrified if she had suggested it to him. That had been her responsibility.

The kitten had taken to the dropper eagerly and hungrily, her small stomach filling, much to Claire's relief.

She was going to be a real *femme fatale*, Claire decided, a natural flirt, and deserved to be named accordingly. As a temporary home for her, Claire had filled an old shoe-box with some soft cotton, and the kitten was now curled up asleep in it. As she watched her Claire tried not to think about how disapproving John would have been about her introduction to the household.

'Just remember,' she told the sleeping creature firmly, 'the drawing room is out of bounds.'

She could have sworn that in her sleep the kitten smiled a knowing, naughty feline smile.

John might not have approved of pets but she had always wanted one, Claire admitted to herself. Already just watching the small sleeping creature made her feel happy.

Happy...that was it. She was going to call her Felicity, she decided. Felicity. She said the name out loud, her smile turning into a small bubble of laughter as the kitten opened her eyes and stretched out her small body as though in approval of her new name.

A telephone call to a friend who had cats of her own had provided her with the name of a vet, and she now walked over to the calendar hanging on the wall to make a note of the appointment she had made for Felicity, plus a note of her follow-up appointment six weeks later, and as she did her attention was caught by the red cross she had placed on the calendar to mark her lunch-date with Poppy and Star.

Well, she certainly wasn't going to have any difficulty in keeping to their agreement to resist the supposed power of their contact with the bride's bouquet.

It would, of course, be different for the other two, or at least she hoped it would be. Poppy would eventually get over her teenage infatuation for her cousin and be able to put it aside and recognise it for what it was, leaving her free to give her adult love to a man who loved her in return.

Star's past history meant that it would not be easy for her to allow herself to trust anyone enough to form a commitment to them... Difficult, but not impossible, and Claire sincerely hoped that she would one day be able to do so.

Beneath that determined front of independence that Star wore so challengingly and fiercely, Claire suspected that there was still a part of her that was very much the lonely, unhappy little girl who had seen her parents destroy one relationship after another and, with them, her security and her belief in the capability of adults to genuinely love one another.

Claire had gone along with their vow to remain unmarried because she had sensed that they needed her support, but her sincerest hope for both of them was that there would come a day when, out of the security of loving and being loved, they could look back and laugh at the vulnerability and pain which had led them to be so afraid of love.

*   *   *

She was just on the point of returning Felicity to her temporary 'basket', having fed her again, when Brad returned. He was earlier than she had expected and had obviously not forgotten his promise to her—or rather to Felicity—because he came in carrying several packages.

'Found a name for her yet?' he asked as Claire went to let him in, still holding the kitten.

'Felicity,' she informed him, 'because her arrival in my home is most felicitous.'

Unlike mine, Brad reflected wryly. He was not oblivious to the fact that she was not entirely at ease with him and silently cursed Irene for having—he was sure—put pressure on her to have him to stay.

If the arrival in her life of something as small and waif-like as the kitten could make her mouth soften and her eyes warm with so much happiness, it didn't say much for the ability of the man in her life to make her happy, he decided critically. If he were in his shoes...

But he wasn't, he reminded himself, and the shoes he was in at the moment—his own shoes—were pinching just a mite too much for comfort.

His interview with Tim had been every bit as difficult as he had envisaged, with Tim being defensive and pessimistic. He preferred a situation where he could praise rather than blame; it got better results faster and, even more important, it helped to keep the sick-pay down. In his opinion, good self-esteem was the best incentive scheme that any workforce—any man—could have.

'Something smells good,' he commented to Claire as he put his packages down on the kitchen table and watched her replace the now sated kitten back in its box.

'It's beef-steak pie,' she told him, lifting her chin, the words almost a challenge. 'I suppose you'd have probably preferred a pot-roast or some pumpkin pie,' she added.

Ah... Brad thought; he now understood the reason for the challenge and the firm determination of that tilted chin.

Hiding a grin, he told her gravely, 'Well, now...that would depend... The kinda pumpkin pie and pot-roast I'm used to, I guess it would be pretty hard for you to serve...'

Claire glared at him in indignation. What was he trying to say? That she wasn't a competent enough cook to make his precious national food?

She opened her mouth to refute his claim firmly and then saw the laughter warming his eyes and paused.

'Go on,' she invited him grimly, letting him know that she wanted to be let in on the joke.

The gleam of amusement became open, rueful laughter as he recongised that she had realised that he was teasing her. That was something he had missed when the kids had been growing up—someone to share his own more mature amusement...his laughter and sometimes his tears at their learning mistakes... Someone to share... Someone just to share his life, he acknowledged— someone like Claire who could recognise when he was deliberately baiting her... Someone like Claire...

Hastily he dragged his thoughts back under control.

'Well, you see, back home the girls kinda cut their milk teeth, in the cooking sense, on pot-roast and pumpkin pie, although, to be fair to my four sisters, mostly they've already had some experience of watching their moms cooking it before they're let loose on the real thing. Have you ever actually eaten charred pot-roast?' he asked her, adding feelingly, 'Four times...and that was just for starters...'

Claire started to laugh. She could well remember her own early attempts at cooking, and Sally's.

'Oh, no, poor you,' she said, her own mirth overcoming her instinctive sympathy as she started to laugh again.

'You can laugh,' Brad complained. 'I sure as hell feel I'm lucky to still have my own teeth ... That's my side of the story,' he told her, and then asked softly, 'So, what's yours? What is it you've got against pot-roast?'

He had caught her off guard with no easy excuse at hand, and after an agitated hesitation she admitted reluctantly, 'Irene wanted me to cook it for you. She brought me this book of American recipes she had borrowed from someone. She thought it would make you feel ... more at home ...'

Aware of Claire's small, tell-tale pause before completing her explanation, Brad guessed that it was her husband's job which Irene had been concerned with rather than his stomach. But he couldn't blame her for that. There was nothing wrong in being a loyal wife.

Brad glanced round the kitchen. In every room of the house bar this one he had been immediately and intensely aware that this was another man's home, and if he felt conscious of that fact then how much more conscious must Claire be that this was, in reality, still another woman's home? How had she lived with that knowledge? he wondered. How had she managed to endure knowing that her husband was still in love with his first wife?

Was *that* why she had become involved with someone else ...? If so, he could scarcely blame her, although ...

'I ... I thought we'd eat in here rather than in the dining room,' he heard Claire saying uncertainly. 'Sally and I always did and—'

'Sure. It's more homely in here,' he agreed calmly. 'But I'll need to shower first; is that OK? I'll only be about ten minutes, but if you give me a shout when you want me...'

Claire could hear him going upstairs as she started to lay the table. She and John had never really laughed together, never shared a sense of humour. John simply hadn't been that kind of man. He had taken life seriously, probably because of Paula's death, Claire acknowledged.

Laughter was supposed to be good for you but it had made her feel rather odd, she decided. She felt slightly dizzy, light-headed almost—'giddy', her great-aunt would have called it disapprovingly. Her mouth curled again and again into a reminiscent smile, an unfamiliar sense of pleasure and light-heartedness filling her.

'I wish Dad would lighten up a bit,' Sally had often complained during her teenage years, and Claire had sympathised with her because her stepdaughter had a wonderful sense of fun.

It must be nice to share that kind of intimacy with someone, Claire decided wistfully as she removed the pie from the oven and put the vegetables into the serving dishes. And they did say, didn't they, that laughter was the best aphrodisiac? Her heart gave a tiny little flutter, the heat from the oven making her face flush.

How much longer would Brad be...? It was over fifteen minutes since he had gone upstairs; perhaps she'd better go and give him that call.

As she walked along the landing she saw that the door to the master bedroom was open. Without thinking she stepped up to it and then paused. Brad's shirt lay on the bed, his shoes beside it on the floor, his trousers over the back of a chair, which meant that Brad, wherever he was, must be minus those articles.

She swallowed a small gulp of panic as the bathroom door opened and Brad walked into the bedroom before she had time to escape.

'Sorry. I'm running late, I know,' he apologised, apparently as oblivious to her flushed face as he was to the fact that all he was wearing was a short—a very short—towelling robe, secured so loosely around his waist that Claire was terrified when he lifted his hands to towel-dry his damp hair that it was going to come unfastened.

Unlike her, he was clearly no stranger to the intimacy of sharing his bedroom with a member of the opposite sex. She and John had very early in the days of their marriage established a routine which ensured that they went to bed at separate times, after allowing one another a decent amount of time and privacy in which to prepare for bed.

Claire suspected that it had been simply for the sake of convention and Sally that John had allowed her to share his room and his bed, and she had sensed his relief when, at the onset of his serious illness, she had suggested that she move into the spare room.

She was still standing just inside the door of Brad's room, transfixed, dizzied almost by the greedy fervour with which she was drinking in the sight of his barely clad body. A hot rush of shame flooded through her as she realised what she was doing. Quickly she turned away, stumbling back out on to the landing.

As a teenager, partially because of her upbringing and partially, she always assumed, because of her own nature, she had been rather naïve and slow to reach sexual awareness, but even when she had her daydreams had been more of the idealised, romantic variety—of meeting someone with whom she would fall in love and marry.

The actual physical details of her lover-to-be had never been something she had dwelt specially upon, and, unlike other girls she had known, she had certainly never drooled over bare male torsos or compared the rival attractions of a pair of well-muscled, strong male arms with an equally well-muscled and strong pair of male buttocks.

Nor had she ever thought about men—or even one specific man—in any sexual sense in the years since, so it was all the more of a shock now to realise that, when she had been standing there watching Brad as he moved lazily and easily around the room, in her mind's eye he had somehow or other disposed of his towelling robe and the Brad she had been watching had been totally and magnificently—very magnificently, she blushed to recall—male.

'That was wonderful,' Brad said when he had finished eating. 'Irene mentioned that you'd be able to introduce me as a temporary member at your local health club. I'm certainly going to need to go if you keep feeding me like this.'

He didn't look as though he needed to work out to her, Claire reflected, but then she had no idea what kind of lifestyle he normally lived; perhaps he exercised regularly at home.

'I must admit I've been a bit lax about developing a proper exercise programme,' he told her, answering her unspoken question. 'But when the kids were younger we lived a pretty outdoors lifestyle, especially in the summer. We'd be out on the lake most summer evenings and weekends, swimming or sailing...'

'The lake?' Claire asked him enviously. She had always had a secret dream of living close to water. As a child it had fascinated her, and a boating holiday—any kind of boating holiday—was her idea óf heaven, although the only time she had persuaded John to hire a boat their holiday hadn't been too successful. John had preferred luxury hotels but she and Sally had had a wonderful time.

'Mmm . . . the town is close by the edge of a lake and most folks locally spend a lot of their recreation time either in it or on it. We had a sailing dinghy and—'

'I've always longed to be able to sail,' Claire told him impulsively, and then flushed slightly. It was unlike her to be so forthcoming with someone.

'Well, there's no reason why you shouldn't learn,' Brad told her.

Claire shook her head. 'Not at my age,' she told him quietly.

'Your age?' Brad scoffed. 'You can't be a day over twenty-seven, if that.'

'Well, I'm thirty-four in actual fact,' Claire informed him quietly, but inwardly she acknowledged that it was flattering that he had mistakenly thought her so much younger.

'Just because we're not under twenty-one any more, it doesn't mean that we can't still have dreams,' Brad told her softly. 'In fact sometimes the older we get, the more we need them.'

He paused, and Claire knew instinctively that he was thinking about a dream of his own. What was it? she wondered curiously.

'I've got this boat out on the lake; four years I've been working on her, stripping down the engines, making her seaworthy. I had this plan that once all the kids were off my hands I'd have some space in my life to do the things I want to do. I had this idea that I'd get the boat ready and that I'd then take off, sail wherever the tide and mood took me . . .'

'Why haven't you?' Claire asked him quietly.

'I got outsmarted by two wily old men—my uncles,' he told her drily. 'I was just on the point of telling them that I wanted out of the company when they beat me to it by announcing that they were both planning to retire— You don't want to hear all this,' he told Claire abruptly.

Yes, I do. I want to hear all about you...know all about you. Claire felt herself going rigid with shock as the words formed silently in her head but thankfully remained unuttered.

'What about you? What are your plans for your future?' Brad asked her, obviously wanting to change the subject.

'I...I...don't really have any,' Claire admitted reluctantly. 'I've got my work at the school, although...'

'Although what?' Brad pressed her as she paused and frowned.

'There's a strong chance that it may have to close. Lack of funding,' Claire explained.

'Then what will you do?' Brad asked.

Claire shook her head. 'I'm not sure, although it is always possible to find some kind of voluntary work even if...'

'Even if it's not exactly what you might want to choose,' Brad supplied for her. 'What would you prefer to do?'

'I like working with children,' Claire confessed. 'There's something about their hope and optimism, even those...'

'You obviously love them,' Brad told her.

'Because they are easy to love,' Claire responded. 'And they have so much love to give...'

She should have had children of her own, Brad decided; she was that kind of woman—intensely loving and maternal in the very best sense of the word, and if he could recognise that then surely her late husband must have done too, so why...?

Their conversation was getting too intimate, too close to subjects that she didn't want to discuss, Claire recognised, quickly getting up from the table, saying that it was getting late, that they still hadn't discussed the terms of his stay with her.

CHAPTER SIX

BRAD was not in a very good mood. He had just spent the morning going over the books and checking through the order book and it was obvious to him that things were in an even worse financial mess than he had predicted.

The sensible thing to do would be simply to cancel the franchise, close it down as a loss-maker and cut their losses. But if he did that...

How would Claire react to the fact that he was putting Tim out of a job—and why should he care?

He leaned back in his borrowed chair in his borrowed office—Tim's office, in fact—and closed his eyes, considering his options.

If they made some improvements, tightened things up, developed a more aggressive selling stance and pulled in some more orders, there was a small—a very small— chance that they might be able to turn things around. But achieving that, meeting all those objectives—and they would have to meet them—would require some brutally demanding hard work and the kind of dedication that was synonymous with the term 'workaholic'. The kind of man that Tim just was not—at the moment!

It would mean recruiting a new agent, someone who could motivate the self-employed fitters who installed the units to adapt the same positive, speedy approach to their work that the firm looked for in its American fitters. Mentally he reviewed the personnel on their home-base payroll. There was someone who could take on such a challenge—on a short-term basis—but how would Tim react to having someone brought in over his head?

The company needed a very different kind of management approach from the one it presently had if it was to survive and succeed.

Tim . . . Claire's brother-in-law . . . and her lover?

Brad closed his eyes again and expelled a weary sigh.

He had heard Claire coming upstairs last night shortly after eleven; he had still been working and had, in fact, gone on working until after midnight.

When she slept in her solitary bed in her solitary room did she dream of her lover? Did she lie awake thinking of him, aching for him, as he . . .?

He tensed and sat up as he heard the office door open.

'Ah, Tim. No, it's all right; come in. I wanted to have a chat with you anyway.'

'But at least nothing's been said about any redundancy yet,' Claire tried to console Tim.

'No, but it can only be a matter of time,' he predicted gloomily.

Claire watched him sympathetically. He had arrived half an hour earlier looking for Brad, who had apparently left him just before lunch without giving any indication of where he was going.

'I thought he might have come back here,' Tim had told her when she had shaken her head in answer to his initial query.

Much as Claire sympathised—and she did—there was not a lot that she could say and even less that she could do other than listen to him as he paced her kitchen and unburdened himself to her.

She sensed that Tim had been half hoping that Brad might have confided his plans for Tim's future to her and in a sense she was relieved that he had not; it spared her from either having to betray his confidence or withhold valuable information from Tim.

'Everything's changed so much,' Tim told her miserably. 'You've got to be so much more competitive, so much more aggressive, and I'm too old to learn those sorts of tricks. And God knows where I'm going to find another job at my age...'

He grimaced as the kitten started to wail. 'She'll scratch your furniture to ribbons,' he warned Claire.

'No, she won't,' Claire contradicted him serenely. 'I'm going to get her a scratching-post.'

'Mmm...' Tim eyed the kitten doubtfully. He knew how Irene would have reacted if he had turned up with it at home, but then Irene had never been as soft-hearted as Claire. In many ways Irene was very like her brother.

'Look, I'd better go,' he told Claire. 'Brad's probably back by now and wondering where on earth I am.'

'I'll see you out to your car,' Claire offered.

He looked tired and stressed, a bit like a slightly rumpled, unhappy teddy bear, Claire decided affectionately as they made their way outside.

'Thanks for listening to me,' he told her gruffly. 'I suppose if I'm honest I've known for a while that things can't go on the way they are, but one always hopes.'

Poor Tim.

'Try not to worry,' Claire advised him, reaching out to hug him affectionately.

As he drove down the road towards Claire's house Brad saw the two of them locked in a deep embrace, oblivious to his approach.

They broke apart, Tim turning to get into his car without looking behind him, and Claire remained on the footpath watching his car disappear, only aware of

Brad's arrival when he slammed his car door. She turned to face him with a startled expression.

'Oh, Brad... You've just missed Tim,' she began. 'He—'

'Yes, I saw him,' Brad said tersely.

Claire tensed, searching Brad's averted profile anxiously as she recognised his curt withdrawal.

Was Tim right? Was Brad on the point of dismissing him? She knew that there was no way she could bring herself to ask him; all she could manage was a hesitant, 'Did you want to speak to Tim...?'

'Not right now,' he told her grimly, walking away from her and heading towards the house, leaving her to follow him—an act which in itself was so out of character for him that it caught her off guard. One of the first things she had noticed about him and reluctantly liked had been his quietly considerate good manners, his way of treating a woman with the kind of old-fashioned courtesy which seemed to have gone out of fashion.

'In fact, right now, I think it would be just as well if I didn't speak to him,' he threw at her over his shoulder as he reached the back door.

'You're... you're angry with him...' Claire guessed hesitantly.

'Angry with him! That's one way of putting it,' Brad agreed bitingly as he waited for her to precede him into the kitchen.

'I know... he is very anxious about his job...' Claire revealed, stumbling slightly over the words, wondering if she was doing the wrong thing in saying them. 'Tim may not be a particularly... ambitious or aggressive man,' Claire told him, feeling that she ought to do something to defend her brother-in-law and draw attention to his good points, 'but he *is* very conscientious, very—'

'*You* obviously hold him in high esteem,' Brad interrupted her.

The sarcasm in his voice made Claire feel uncomfortable.

'You obviously think I'm trying to interfere in something that is none of my business,' she felt bound to say, 'but—'

'But you'd like to know anyway what my plans are for the future of the British side of our distribution network and, of course, Tim's future with it. Is that it?' Brad asked her, and grimly continued before she could make any denial.

'Very well, I'll tell you. Some changes will very definitely have to be made. As you yourself have just said, Tim is not the most confident of men and his lack of assertiveness comes across to potential customers as a lack of confidence, not just in himself but in our product as well. Couple that with his apparent inability to recruit the kind of highly motivated and even more highly skilled technicians and fitters we pride ourselves on using back home and it's no wonder we're having the problems over here that we are having.'

'So, you *do* mean to cancel your contract with him and find a new distributor?' Claire challenged him.

To her surprise, instead of immediately conceding that she was right, Brad frowned slightly and then said slowly, 'No, not necessarily.'

When Claire looked questioningly at him, he explained, 'It occurs to me that Tim might benefit from an intensive course on self-assertion techniques plus some input from a more positive role model to show him—'

'How the job *should* be done,' Claire supplied wryly.

'No,' Brad corrected her quietly. 'To show him what *can* be achieved with a more positive approach...a different outlook if you like. We have someone working for us on the distribution side back home who would be perfect for the job, although it won't be easy persuading him to come over here. But that's my problem and you aren't interested in my problems, are you? Only Tim's. But then, after all, you are lovers.'

'*Lovers*?' Claire repeated in astonishment.

But before she could continue Brad was demanding angrily, 'When did it start? After your husband's death...? Before it?'

An affair! Brad thought she was having an affair with *Tim*.

'OK, I can understand that your... marriage may not have...satisfied you, but hell...surely a woman like you could have found a man who was free to have a relationship and not one...'

Claire stared at him in shocked disbelief. 'You have no right to make those kinds of assumptions about me,' she told him stiffly. 'You know nothing about me... or about my marriage.'

Even though she would rather have died than admit it to him, his comment about her marriage had hit a painful nerve, but not for the reason that he imagined.

'I would never have an affair,' she told him with passionate sincerity. 'Never... I couldn't.'

The vehemence in her voice fuelled Brad's fury. How could she deny it when he had seen the evidence with his own eyes, heard it with his own ears? And if she had to have an affair with someone, surely she could have found someone more...more worthy than her poor, downtrodden brother-in-law?

'"Couldn't"?' he challenged her contemptuously. 'Oh, come on. You're an adult, mature woman; you've been married... Your body knows how it feels to experience sexual desire, sexual fulfilment...sexual need; you must—'

'No,' Claire protested frantically. 'No, that's impossible; I could never... I have never...'

Something in her voice, in her face made Brad pause and look searchingly at her. She looked haunted, her eyes shadowed, her voice shamed... bruised.

'What is it?' he asked her. 'What is it you're trying to say?'

'Nothing,' Claire denied rigidly, starting to turn away from him.

But he reached out and caught hold of her arm, preventing her, telling her, 'No, you can't leave it like that. You could never... have never... what?' he pressed.

He could feel the slight tremor that she tried to suppress run down her arm as she refused to look at him.

It was no use, Claire acknowledged fatalistically. Brad wasn't going to give up until she had told him the truth. She closed her eyes, fighting back the engulfing wave of panic that threatened her. How on earth had this happened? How on earth had she got herself in such a situation, betrayed herself to such an extent?

As a child she had learned that the easiest way to deal with her aunt's displeasure whenever she provoked it was simply to take a deep breath and submit to it, rather like taking a nasty dose of medicine all in one big swallow, so that she could get the whole thing over and done with.

'I could *never* take a lover, have *never* had a lover,' she emphasised with quiet dignity, fiercely ignoring her voice's struggle not to wobble and the fact that she knew that her face, her whole body in fact, was burning with humiliated colour as she made herself admit the shameful truth to him—not that he had any right to demand it or any right to make her reveal it...

'John... our marriage... John married me because he wanted a stepmother for Sally. I knew... he told me... that he could never love anyone the way he had

loved Paula, but that for Sally's sake he felt that he ought
to provide her with a substitute mother.'

'And you were happy with that...you accepted that?'
Brad persisted. There was something here that he didn't
understand. Had she, perhaps, been so desperately in
love with her husband that she had hoped that he would
change his mind...that he would fall in love with *her*?
His heart ached with pity for her, and anger as well.

'Yes,' Claire confirmed.

'But why?' Brad probed. 'Why? Why marry a man
who you knew did not love you? A man who could never
be a proper husband to you...never give you
children...never share with you the pleasure of sexual
fulfilment and commitment, the emotional...' He paused
as he saw the way she shuddered at his mention of her
lack of sexual fulfilment.

'What is it?' he asked her curiously. 'What's wrong?'

'I didn't mind the fact that John only wanted me as
a stepmother for Sally because I didn't *want* to have a
sexual relationship with him...or with anyone,' she told
him doggedly.

For a long moment they looked at one another.

'You didn't want a sexual relationship...with anyone,'
Brad repeated.

Something here was eluding him. There had been no
sexual revulsion or rejection in her reaction to him
when... Shock, yes...anger too. Shock, anger and
arousal. He listed them carefully in his mind a second
and then a third time just to be sure that he was not
making a mistake and letting his own emotions and responses obscure hers.

He looked away from her and started to release her
arm, too stunned by what she had said to know what to
say or do, and then he looked briefly back at her and

saw that her eyes were brimming with huge tears which she was struggling desperately to control.

'Oh, hell, come here,' he muttered roughly under his breath, reacting instinctively to her distress, reaching for her and wrapping her in his arms in a fiercely protective hug, rocking her against his body as he held her tight with one arm and smoothed the silky fineness of her hair with the other and tried to comfort her.

'It's OK... It's OK,' he told her gruffly. 'I'm sorry as hell that I upset you. I didn't... What I said was out of line.

'Talk to me, Claire,' he groaned as he felt her body tensing under her attempts to stifle her sobs. 'Talk to me... Let it all out... Tell me what it's all about.'

'I can't,' Claire sobbed. 'I can't...'

'Yes, you can... Of course you can... Whatever it is you can tell me...' Brad crooned the words in much the same way as he had once crooned similar reassurances to his brothers and sisters, comforting them through their childhood woes. Only Claire wasn't a child, and she certainly wasn't one of his siblings; his body was telling him that much.

Claire, thank the Lord, was too caught up in her own emotions to be aware of his arousal.

'Tell me,' he insisted, and then added with a smile, 'I shan't let you go until you do.'

'There was a man,' Claire told him reluctantly. 'Another graduate. Three of us were sharing a rented house. It was my first time away from home... I...I suppose I was very naïve... My great-aunt was very strict; I...I didn't have very much experience, didn't know...

'He...he came to my room. He said the gas in his own meter had run out and he had no money to replenish it. He asked if he could study with me... He offered to make our supper... I...I had just had a bath...

Our rooms were very cold and I was wearing my...my nightdress and my dressing gown... I didn't know... I didn't think.

'I...I went over to my bookshelves to get a book I needed. He followed me over. He was standing behind me... He put his arms round me...' Claire moistened her upper lip, her eyes darkening as she relived what had happened.

'At first I was too surprised to realise... I thought...I asked him to let me go but he wouldn't; he just laughed. He started...he started...' She stopped and swallowed painfully.

'He started to kiss the side of my neck.' She gave a small shudder. 'I didn't want him to... I tried to move away but he wouldn't let me go. He started pulling at my dressing gown and...' Her voice faltered to a standstill.

Brad's arm tightened slightly around her. 'It's OK. Take your time,' he told her softly.

'I... Well, I'm sure you can guess the rest. He thought that by agreeing to him coming in I was...I was agreeing to have sex with him. He was furious with me when I refused—told me...called me...I...I thought he was going to force me...rape me...

'We struggled for a while and eventually I managed to get free. I ran out of the house and into the street. It was raining and I slipped on the wet pavement... John saw me...he was on his way home... He stopped his car and came to help me. When I felt him touch me, at first I thought... I was almost hysterical,' she admitted huskily, and Brad, remembering the night when *he* had unwittingly pursued her down a wet street, winced inwardly and cursed himself.

'Eventually he managed to calm me down and make me explain. He took me home with him…made me stay the night.

'He was so kind to me, so… so caring… I felt so safe with him,' she told Brad quietly. 'So… it was easy being with him and Sally, who, coincidentally was a pupil at the school where I was placed for teaching practice. There was no pressure… no awful feeling that he was about to pounce on me… that I might somehow… that he might think…'

Claire gave a tiny, despairing shake of her head.

'You must think me very stupid, very naïve… to be so afraid of… of giving the wrong impression, of having someone, some man think… But I'd never felt very comfortable with boys… My great-aunt… And sexually…'

She struggled to find the right words and could only say huskily, 'I didn't… Some people don't… The fact that John didn't want to consummate our marriage was never a problem for me, and before you make any more accusations,' she told him, a little more fiercely, 'I was never tempted to break the vow of… of fidelity which I'd made when we were married. You must find me very… very cowardly and…'

'No,' Brad denied. 'In actual fact I think you're very brave to have told me what you just have,' he elucidated gently when she looked uncertainly at him.

What he couldn't tell her was what he thought of her husband, a man whom she obviously still looked up to but who, as far as he was concerned, had cruelly and selfishly taken advantage of her by using her naïvety and insecurity to trap her into a marriage which had robbed her of any right to discover her own sexuality.

'How old were you when you and John married?' he asked her gently.

'Twenty-two,' Claire told him.

Twenty-two. His heart ached for her.

'Don't look at me like that,' she cried out fiercely when she saw his face. 'I don't want your pity. I wanted to marry John... I wanted...'

'To deny your sexuality. Yes, I know,' Brad said.

'Some people... some women just aren't very highly sexually motivated,' Claire protested defensively. 'They just don't feel...'

'Some women... some men are born with only a very low sex drive,' Brad agreed, 'but you aren't one of them,' he told her positively.

Claire stared at him, her eyes rounding, her face starting to flush slightly.

'How can you say that?' she protested. 'You don't know—'

'Oh, I know,' Brad interrupted. 'I know very well because of this...'

And then, before she could really grasp what was happening, he had tightened his hold around her, one hand behind her head, and fastened his mouth gently over hers in the lightest and most delicate of kisses until the tantalising brush of his mouth against her own made her reach up instinctively to pull him down closer so that her lips could touch his fully, her body melting in liquid pleasure into his as he started to kiss her properly.

How could she ever have believed that she didn't want this? Claire marvelled dizzily as her body threw off the shackles of self-restraint and fear and gloried unashamedly in its need to press even closer to Brad's.

It was like taking off dark sunglasses and suddenly being dazzled by the brilliance of the sun, Claire decided in dazed euphoria as her senses revelled in their untrammelled freedom to indulge themselves.

The sound of Brad's breathing, heavy and uneven, the smell of his skin, the heat of his body... Greedily Claire's senses absorbed each new, sensual discovery, each new, sensual pleasure, whilst her mouth clung hungrily to his, willingly obeying his tongue's urgent demand for her to part her closed lips to allow it to dart inside with quick, urgent strokes.

She could feel the harshness of Brad's chest against her breasts as he started to breathe more deeply. The stiffness of the cloth separating their bodies chaffed their unfamiliar tenderness.

She could feel the difference, the arousal in her breasts, her nipples, her whole body, Claire realised.

And she could feel too the arousal in Brad's. But where once the knowledge of a man's arousal had filled her with revulsion and fear now her body shivered with heady, feminine triumph at her ability to cause such a reaction.

The discovery of her own sensuality and of Brad's reaction to it was like drinking a heady aphrodisiac. She almost felt drunk on the effects of what she was experiencing, Claire recognised in a daze of pleasure as, without even knowing what she was doing, she rubbed her body provocatively against Brad's, opening her eyes to gaze drowsily into his, her pupils so dilated that Brad caught his breath in an instantaneous and intense surge of sexual urgency.

She didn't know what she was doing, he suspected as he fought to control his own searingly intense desire. Not to herself and certainly not to him. Oh, she knew that he was aroused but she didn't know, had no way of knowing, just how out of character it was for him to be so vulnerable to sexual desire or just how fiercely intense that desire was.

She was still looking up at him, her mouth open over his, her teeth tugging sensually at his bottom lip, and he wondered what she would say if he told her how damned close he was to making the most primitive and urgent sensual use of the table only inches behind them.

And somehow he knew that the way he was feeling right now, the way she was unconsciously telling him what she was feeling...satisfying each other once wasn't going to be enough... No way was it going to be enough.

As he tried to stifle the groan of longing that her teasingly erotic movements against his body were causing, he caught sight of the kitchen clock and cursed under his breath as he saw the time.

The office was twenty minutes' drive away and he had an appointment in exactly half an hour with a potential customer.

'Claire...' He whispered her name into her mouth, watching in aching regret as he saw her eyes start to cloud. 'Claire...I've got to go,' he murmured softly.

He'd got to go... But he couldn't go... She needed him, wanted him.

'No...' Claire started to protest huskily, and then abruptly she realised what she was doing, what she was saying, the enormity of her own behaviour. Scarlet-faced with mortification, she pulled away from him, unable even to look at him, never mind actually meet his eyes as she heard him explaining that he had an appointment but that he would get back just as soon as he could.

'There was no need for you to...to do what you just did,' she told him in a suffocated voice. 'I know you feel sorry for me and that...'

Brad cursed silently, realising what she was thinking and what she was probably feeling. She thought that he had made love to her out of pity.

'Claire—'

'I suppose it must be quite a change for a man like you. I suppose I've got a certain curiosity value, if nothing else. After all, there can't be many women of thirty-four in this day and age who don't...who've never...'

'Claire, don't,' he begged her. 'You're wrong. It wasn't—'

'They used to be good music-hall fodder, didn't they—middle-aged virgins, repressed, dried up, fossilised...?'

He could hear in her voice the tears she wouldn't let fall and he ached to reach out and take hold of her, but she was already stepping back from him, her eyes wild and angry, warning him not to come any closer.

'This is all my own fault,' Claire told him bitterly. 'I should never have given in to Irene and agreed to let you stay here. I never wanted—' She stopped but Brad knew what she had been going to say.

'You never wanted me here in the first place,' he guessed wryly.

'Why can't you all leave me alone to live my life the way I want to?' she demanded fiercely. 'You... Irene...even Sally with that ridiculous trick to force us to catch her bouquet. As though anyone gives any credence to that ridiculous superstition these days...'

'What superstition?' Brad asked her curiously.

'The one that says the girl who catches the bride's bouquet will be the next to marry,' Claire told him angrily. 'Sally arranged it so that both of her bridesmaids and I were tricked into catching it. She even put something about it on her postcard.'

The postcard... Suddenly Brad understood. So that was what the reference to Claire having a part-share in a man had meant.

Claire glowered at him furiously as she saw the way he had started to grin.

'Look, I've got to go,' he reiterated, 'but I *am* coming back, and when I do don't even bother to think about running away, Claire,' he warned her firmly.

'This,' he told her softly, reaching out and touching her lips lightly with his fingertips before she could stop him, 'is just the beginning...'

Claire stared at him, transfixed by the sheer intensity of the jolt of sensation that had run through her at his touch.

She wanted to tell him that he was wrong, that she didn't *want* whatever it was that he thought they had started to continue, but somehow the words just wouldn't come and she had to watch in tongue-tied silence as he headed for the door.

The plaintive mewing of the kitten broke the heavy silence of the kitchen. Claire went automatically to pick her up, stroking the soft baby fur and marvelling at the little creature's capacity to trust and survive as she started to purr noisily.

She was still semi-dazed by disbelief at everything that had happened—not just the intimate physical sensuality she had shared with Brad and her unexpected response to him but, even more unbelievably, the fact that she had actually told him about her past, revealed to him the secret shame and shock she had felt and the way it had affected her whole life and her feelings about herself and her sexuality.

Not even to John had she confided her fear that *she* somehow had been responsible, had invited in some way that young man's assault on her, but somehow it had almost been as though Brad had known what she was thinking, what she was feeling...had known just how to encourage her to reveal that hidden fear to him.

And as for what had happened afterwards... Could it have been the result of the release of all the emotions she had repressed by locking away her fears about what had happened and her dread that she had somehow been responsible for it?

It was a well-known fact that emotional trauma could have an extremely odd effect on human behaviour.

But what about the fact that the night before last she had been dreaming about Brad in the most erotic way?

The kitten gave a sharp howl of protest, making Claire realise that the eye-dropper was empty of milk.

Apologising to her, Claire refilled it, smiling at the way the little creature clung to the dropper with her front paws as she sucked on the teat.

Sally had already told her that she intended to wait until she was at least thirty before she and Chris started their family. She was twenty-five now, which meant that she was going to have a long wait before she became a grandmother, Claire acknowledged.

A grandmother... A rueful, slightly sad smile touched her mouth as she admitted to herself how much she would secretly have liked to have children, a family of which Sally would always have remained her eldest and most specially loved daughter.

It was not too late, of course. Women of her age and even older were having babies every day, many of them without the support of a husband or partner, but, having been brought up solely by her great-aunt, Claire had very ambivalent feelings about having a child on her own. Of course, if she were ever to find herself in a situation where for some reason she'd conceived accidentally, then there would be no question but that she would have her child and love him or her.

She bent her head protectively over the kitten as she realised the direction her thoughts were taking and just why the thought of an accidental pregnancy should have crossed her mind.

It wasn't going to happen, of course. *She* must make sure that it did not happen, she told herself sternly.

Outside it had started to rain, the wind gusting fiercely against the window.

The weather forecast had warned that they were in for a stormy evening with heavy rain and gale-force winds. As she returned Felicity to the new basket that Brad had bought for her and glanced out of the window at the lowering sky, Claire was thankful that she didn't have to go out.

CHAPTER SEVEN

BRAD grimaced in disgust as he realised that one of the tyres on his hire car had developed a slow puncture and was now flat. Cursing under his breath, he glanced from the car window to the bleak, empty landscape and the heavy rain. It was barely six o'clock in the evening but the sky was so overcast that it was already almost dark.

There was no one else around, the desolate area that the local council had designated as a new industrial complex as yet little more than a vast sea of mud, broken here and there by sets of footings.

It had been a chance remark during his interview with their potential new customer—an official from the head office of a locally based insurance broker which was thinking of installing air-conditioning in all its offices— that had led to his trip out here to look at the new industrial site.

He hadn't realised, until the other man had mentioned it, that the existing warehouse was built on a piece of potentially very valuable land. The town had expanded rapidly in the years after the warehouse had first been constructed—adjacent to the original owner's home—and although Brad had been aware that virtually all the property surrounding the warehouse was residential he hadn't appreciated the significance of this fact until the other man had brought it to his attention.

He had a client, he had told Brad, a well-known local builder, who he suspected would be very interested in acquiring the land for development if it ever came onto the market. After he had gone, a few brief enquiries by

117

Brad had elicited the information that as prime residential building land the warehouse site was very good indeed, and, moreover, that if they were to move to a new purpose-built unit the savings they could make would more than offset the cost of such a move.

On impulse Brad had decided to drive out and look at the new industrial complex that the local council were building, but what he hadn't bargained for was the fact that his hire car was going to get a puncture.

It was still raining very heavily but there was no help for it—he was going to have to get out and change that tyre, Brad acknowledged, removing his suit jacket and opening the car door.

Ten minutes later, his hair plastered wetly to his scalp, his back soaked to the skin through the inadequate protection of his shirt, Brad had managed to remove the spare wheel from the trunk—the *boot* of the car, he amended grimly—and to locate the jack.

The unmade road along which he had driven to inspect the site was rapidly changing to a thick mush of sticky mud beneath the lashing downpour. Removing the rubber-backed lining from the boot floor to use as a kneeling pad, Brad started to jack up the car.

Half an hour later, so wet that he might just as well have been standing naked under a shower, and perspiring heavily from his efforts to release the wheel-nuts, Brad gave in. What he wouldn't give now for a can of lubricant, he thought, but the nuts, fitted by machine, were simply not going to budge.

He reached into his car for his phone and punched in the number of the car-hire firm.

It was over an hour and a half before he finally saw the headlights of the breakdown vehicle coming towards him through the heavy downpour of the continuing rain.

He had been reluctant to run the car engine for too long in case he ran out of petrol and his wet shirt, still clinging clammily and coldly to his skin, coupled with the sharp drop in temperature which had accompanied the driving rain made him shiver and sneeze as he stepped out of the car to greet the mechanic.

'Better watch it, mate,' the mechanic told him cheerfully as he sprayed the stubborn wheel-nuts and waited for the lubricant to take effect. 'Sounds like you've got yourself a nasty chill there.'

It was another half an hour before the wheel was finally changed, the wheel-nuts proving recalcitrantly stubborn but eventually coming free.

Thanking the mechanic, Brad climbed back in the car and restarted the engine.

Claire glanced uncertainly at the kitchen clock. Where was Brad? She had assumed, obviously erroneously, that he was going to be back in time for dinner but it was after nine now and she had long since disposed of the meal she had prepared for him.

When Brad hadn't returned when she had expected she had been tempted to phone the office, but she had reminded herself fiercely that he was simply her lodger and that was the only relationship between them—the only relationship she *wanted* there to be between them.

It hadn't been easy to ignore the mocking laughter of the inner voice that had taunted her, Liar, but somehow she had made herself do so. If she'd wanted or needed any confirmation that what had happened between them this afternoon was something that Brad very definitely did not want to take any further, she had surely had it in the very fact that he had delayed his return for so long.

Don't run away, he had told her, but perhaps, like her, he too had been caught up in the intensity of the moment, suspending normal, rational judgement and reality.

Hannah had been round earlier to leave her a book that she had promised to lend her on traditional Edwardian rose gardens; she would make herself a hot drink and go and sit down in the sitting room and look at it, Claire promised herself. She had just settled down when she saw the headlights of Brad's car. Uncertainly she bit her lip, not sure whether to stay where she was or go and greet him.

As his landlady, she ought perhaps at least to check to see if he wanted anything to eat. She was not really sure what the mode of behaviour should be between landlady and lodger—where one drew the line between a presence that was welcoming and one that was intrusive.

It was time to feed Felicity, she reminded herself, and if she didn't appear Brad might think...might assume...

What? she asked herself grimly. That she was afraid...embarrassed...self-conscious? Well, he would be right on all those counts. She did feel all those things and more—much more, she acknowledged, her body suddenly growing hot as she had an unnervingly vivid memory of the way his mouth had felt on hers—his body, his...

Swallowing hard, she reminded herself that, no matter what she felt, she *did* have a responsibility as his landlady to make at least an attempt to behave in a businesslike manner towards him.

Irene would certainly have something to say to her if she learned that Claire had left him supperless. As she got up and walked towards the door Claire heard Brad walk into the hall and sneeze—once and then again.

Frowning now, she opened the door, her eyes widening in shock as she saw his coatless, damply dishevelled state.

'Brad, what on earth...?'

'It's nothing,' he said. 'There was a problem with the car and I had to wait for them to get a breakdown truck out to me. I should have let you know, but I had no idea how long they were going to be.'

A problem. Her heart thumped anxiously against her chest wall. 'Not an accident?' she protested. 'You—'

'No, not an accident,' he assured her. 'I had a flat tyre, that's all, but unfortunately—' he paused for another volley of sneezes, visibly shivering as Claire looked on in appalled consternation— 'I tried to change it myself and got soaked,' he told her ruefully, his teeth suddenly chattering.

'You're soaked,' Claire told him. 'And frozen. You'd better go upstairs and have a hot shower. I'll make you a drink and something to eat.'

Had she got any cold or flu remedy in the house? Claire wondered, listening anxiously as she heard Brad pause halfway up the stairs for another fit of obviously feverish sneezing.

He was going to be lucky if all he got away with was a bad chill, she recognised as she hurried into the kitchen to fill the kettle and look through the drawers to try to unearth the old hot-water bottle she always kept handy for cold sufferers. In these centrally heated days it probably wasn't necessary but somehow it made one feel better, Claire acknowledged. Sally certainly insisted on having it whenever she went down with a cold.

A brief check on the high shelf where she kept her medicines revealed the patent aspirin-based remedy which Sally always swore worked for her. Expelling a small sigh of relief, Claire picked it up. She had no doubt whom Irene would blame if Brad did become ill.

He was used to a much better regulated climate than theirs, she reminded herself as she added some brandy to the mug of coffee that she had made him. He would, perhaps, be better off going straight to bed and keeping warm there rather than coming down for something to eat. She could easily take him a tray of food upstairs.

His bedroom door was ajar when she went up with the coffee but, recalling what had happened the last time she had walked into his room, she paused, knocking and calling out uncertainly.

'Brad...?'

His husky 'Come in' confirmed her earlier suspicions about the state of his health.

'I've brought you some coffee,' she told him, and added, 'And I've put some brandy in it, so...'

'Wonderful,' Brad praised her. He was sitting on the edge of the bed, wearing the towelling robe she had seen him in before. As he reached out to take the coffee from her Claire saw to her concern that his face already looked hectically and feverishly flushed.

'I think you might be running a temperature,' she warned him gently.

'I think you're probably right,' Brad agreed. He was beginning to feel decidedly unwell. As a boy he had been very susceptible to frighteningly severe chest infections brought on by any kind of exposure to a cold or flu virus, but fortunately over the years he seemed to have developed a better immunity to them. Until now, he acknowledged, already recognising the signs of a return of his childhood symptoms.

'You ought to have something to eat,' Claire told him, 'but I don't think you should come back downstairs; you look—'

'I'll be all right,' Brad interrupted her stoically. 'A good night's sleep and a couple more of these ...' he told her, pointing to the brandy-laced coffee she had brought him.

'I could make you an omelette,' Claire offered, but he was shaking his head.

'I don't think I could,' he told her ruefully. 'My throat...' He touched the tender area, wincing as he felt the tell-tale swelling of his glands.

'I've got some aspirin,' Claire said, but Brad shook his head again. 'I'm allergic to it,' he told her wryly. 'Look, I promise you, I'll be fine.'

The concern he could see in her eyes made him realise how tempting it would be to exaggerate his symptoms. If he hadn't been feeling so damn ill and weak there would have been a lot he could have done with that warm, womanly anxious look.

As he shivered involuntarily and started to sneeze again Claire made a soft sound of distress and urged him to get into bed.

'I can't,' he told her.

'You can't? But...'

Since he was already sitting on the side of the bed, Claire was puzzled by his refusal, until he informed her softly, 'In order to get into bed I've got to take this robe off first, and if I do that...' He paused deliberately, and as she unwittingly focused on the bare V of warm brown flesh in front of her, with its soft, tantalising tangle of silky dark hair, she suddenly realised what he meant: that he was naked beneath his robe.

Her soft, betraying 'Oh' and the quick flush of colour that stained her skin made Brad ache to reach out and take hold of her, to pull her down against his body and...

Stop that, he warned himself, stifling a low groan of unexpected arousal. There were some things that even the threat of a feverish chest infection couldn't keep down—quite literally, he realised in wry self-mockery.

'I...I'd better go downstairs,' Claire mumbled awkwardly. 'I was wondering...if you'd like a hot-water bottle,' she added, and then wondered what on earth had made her make such a patently silly offer. He was an adult, not a child, and, unlike Sally, he—

'A hot-water bottle...' Brad closed his eyes and gave a long, appreciative sigh. 'I can't think of anything I'd like more...'

Oh, yes, he could, he corrected himself as he watched Claire disappear. He could think of something he'd quite definitely like very, very much more, and that was holding Claire's body next to his own...a real, live comforter.

Ten minutes later when Claire returned she was concerned to see how much more hectically flushed Brad was, his breathing painfully rasping and laboured. As she leaned across the bed to hand him the hot-water bottle she could feel the feverish heat coming off his body. Concerned, she asked him, 'Would you like me to send for a doctor? Your breathing... I'm—'

'No...I'll be OK,' Brad assured her. 'It sounds worse than it is.'

'Are you sure?' Claire queried doubtfully. 'You—'

'I'm sure,' Brad told her firmly. 'A good night's sleep and I'll be fine.'

It might not strictly speaking be the truth, Brad acknowledged ruefully as he watched Claire walking away from him, waiting until she had closed the door behind her to let his body relax into the racking fit of shivers he had managed to suppress whilst she was there, but he knew these feverish bronchial attacks of old and they always seemed worse to the onlooker than they actually were.

* * *

Claire made an irritated sound of self-criticism as she got out of the bath and remembered that she hadn't locked the back door. Reaching for her towelling robe, she pulled it on over her still damp body, acknowledging that she had better go and do so before she forgot—again.

The back door securely locked, she had almost reached her own bedroom when she heard a noise from Brad's room. She paused, and heard him cry out. Something was wrong.

Quickly she hurried into his room. The bedside lamp was switched on, a glass of water which Brad must have fetched from the bathroom earlier next to it. Brad was lying on his side, facing away from her, muttering something hoarsely under his breath. As Claire strained to hear what it was she automatically reached across the bed towards him, saying his name with anxious urgency.

When he didn't make any response her anxiety increased. She touched his bare shoulders lightly, wincing as she felt the heat coming off his skin, and listened to the harsh bark of his cough. This time he registered her presence, turning over to face her, saying something that she couldn't catch and then calling out sharply, 'No... No... It isn't true... Dad...'

Claire shivered as she heard the pain in his voice and realised that he was talking in his sleep—a very feverish and restless sleep, if the tumbled state of the bedclothes and the low, emotional sound of his voice were anything to go by, she recognised.

Did he dream of his dead parents often, she wondered compassionately as she heard him whisper his father's name a second time, or was this just a side effect of his fever?

As he'd turned over the duvet had slid down his body, exposing his torso, warmly tanned and firmly muscled, but it wasn't sensual feminine appreciation of his maleness that Claire felt most strongly as she looked at him but anxious concern as she saw the sweat-soaked dampness of his body hair and the hectic heat of his skin. She watched as, despite the heat, he started to shiver convulsively, another spasm of the harsh, dry cough she had heard earlier racking his chest so painfully that her own actually seemed to ache in sympathetic response.

Automatically she reached out to pull the duvet back up over him, instinctively soothing him with the kind of low-voiced, gentle comfort she had always given Sally as a child. The intensity of the fever worried her and she regretted not insisting on sending for a doctor earlier.

As she tried to tuck the duvet more securely around him her fingertips accidentally touched his skin. Its heat shocked her, fuelling her anxiety. She placed her hand against his forehead. His skin felt burning hot, his hair soaked with sweat.

He was talking in his sleep again, protesting about something or someone—she couldn't tell.

'It's all right, Brad,' she told him gently. 'Everything is all right.'

'Claire...'

Claire froze as the eyes she had thought closed in a deep, fever-fuelled sleep abruptly opened, their gaze focusing on and then fusing hypnotically with hers.

Claire found herself becoming slightly breathless and dizzy as she tried to wrench her eyes away from the hot, mesmerising glitter of Brad's and discovered that she could not do so.

'Claire,' he said again, his voice lower, huskier, the sound of her name something between a growl and a groan. Then he said huskily, 'You're here... I thought you were just a dream... Come closer.'

'No, Brad, you don't...' Claire started to protest, but with surprising strength Brad reached for her, one hand encircling her wrist, the other wrapping around her as he sat up and half lifted and half pulled her with firm insistence onto the bed next to him.

'I thought you were just a dream,' he whispered throatily as his hands framed her face. 'But you're not. You're actually here, and real... very, very real.'

Claire knew that she should say something, do something, but somehow she couldn't, didn't, her body shocked into immobility as Brad breathed the last three words against her lips before gently brushing his own against hers in a kiss that was so tenderly sweet with gentle promise that Claire felt her whole body ache with yearning for him.

This was no brutal, selfish assault on her body, fuelled by a male sexual desire that was completely without emotion or any recognition of her as a person, a woman with needs and emotions of her own.

This was the kiss of a man who knew, who understood, who even in what Claire could only suppose was some fever-induced physical desire for her was still carefully tender and mindful of her vulnerability.

Claire could feel her body start to tremble as Brad cupped her face in his hands and continued to caress her lips with his, brushing gently over them again and again until they felt softly moist, pliantly eager for a more lingering and intense caress.

Without knowing that she had done so Claire moved closer to him, her lips parting on a small breath of shocked pleasure as she heard the low sound of hungry need that Brad made deep in his throat.

She could feel the sensual stroke of his fingertips against her skin as he massaged the delicate flesh behind her ear, his mouth leaving hers briefly as he looked down into her eyes, and then returning to it to kiss her with fierce passion—once and then a second time and then a third, until, unable to bear to be without the hungry contact of his mouth on hers, Claire reached up and wrapped her arms around him, holding him tightly, making small moaning sounds of pleasure deep in her own throat, her whole body on fire, trembling with the aching need she felt for him.

Like someone in a trance, Claire watched him as he released her and gently eased the robe back off her shoulders, her skin as hot and flushed as his as she saw the look in his eyes when his gaze caressed the slender nakedness of her upper body—her slim, narrow shoulders, the creamy smoothness of her skin, the round fullness of her breasts, her nipples flushed and flauntingly erect.

No man had ever seen her naked body before. He watched her with such obviously skin-tingling, erotic thoughts and in such a way, with such an expression in his eyes, that she instinctively responded to his subtle message and to the full-blooded male approval and appreciation of his lingering appraisal of her by arching her spine slightly, her eyelids dropping to conceal her own expression as she watched him back with parted lips and the sure, delicious knowledge that he found her desirable—and, more, that as a man he was just slightly enthralled, slightly and satisfyingly in awe of her womanhood.

It was a heady, aphrodisiac, potent mixture of new emotions for a woman whose only previous feelings towards her sexuality had been a corrosive blend of shame and self-judgement.

Nothing in the way Brad watched her made her feel ashamed. Nothing in the way he looked at her, nothing in the expression in his eyes, made her feel self-conscious or ill at ease, but her mind only absorbed these facts distantly, her senses, her emotions, her concentration focused instead on the way her body was responding to the subtle signs of sexual responsiveness to her in his.

Something about the way his chest rose and fell with increased urgency made her muscles tighten with delicious awareness.

Something about the hot, fiercely controlled smoulder in the way he looked at her mouth and then her breasts and tried not to flooded her body with feminine arousal and pride.

And, most especially, something about the way he moved the lower half of his body beneath the bedclothes, protectively and oh, so betrayingly trying discreetly to bundle the thickness of the duvet cover over the betraying, strong jut of flesh that it couldn't quite disguise made her smile a soft smile of secret pleasure and power to herself.

She deliberately leaned forward to kiss delicately first one and then the other corner of his mouth before teasingly circling the whole outline of his lips with her tongue-tip, her weight supported on the splayed hand she had oh, so accidentally placed provocatively between his open thighs.

Claire had never behaved with such sensual aggression before—had never dreamed that she could, never mind that she would actually want to and, even more mind-stretching, take actual pleasure in doing so.

The reason why she had come into Brad's bedroom was forgotten; the slow, hungry way he had kissed her had seen to that. It wasn't just her mouth that he had sensitised and aroused with his shatteringly erotic kisses, it was her mind, her emotions, her senses and her whole body.

She felt as though she was wrapped in a soft, sensual cloud of physical and emotional pleasure—a sensation both so elusive and so intense that it couldn't be examined or analysed, simply accepted and enjoyed.

The slow groan that built up in Brad's throat as she teased his mouth made her shiver with delicious pleasure, her eyes narrowing to soft, cat-like slits that made his darken to a fiery furnace of strong male desire as she focused on them.

His hand lifted to her throat, slowly stroking it, his thumb on the pulse, flooding her body with heat as her breathing deepened and quickened in response to his reaction to her.

Claire could feel her breasts swelling and tightening, and somewhere on the edge of her awareness she was conscious of a small sense of outraged shock from her real self that this new, sensual and very wanton part of her should take such obvious self-confident feminine delight in his reaction.

Her body tautened and arched with provocative sensuality, silently calling to Brad to absorb visually the effect that he was having on her and to respond to it by reaching out to stroke and caress the warm, taut flesh so tantalisingly within his reach and yet at the same time denied to him as Claire copied his own, earlier caress, cupping his face in both her hands, gently holding him slightly away from her body as she started to kiss him.

There was a wonderful sense of control and power in knowing how much he wanted her and yet knowing at the same time that he wouldn't break the gentle restriction that she had placed on him. A sense, too, of wanting to push him that little bit further, of wanting to test just how much he did want her, of wanting to prove to herself that his desire for her was just as fiercely intense as hers for him.

She heard the sound of frustrated protest that he made deep in his throat, a thrill of sensual excitement running down her spine as he suddenly turned the tables on her, taking control of the kiss from her, the swift thrust of his tongue between her open lips making her shudder in heated arousal, her body softening, swaying closer to his as though the flushed, hard tips of her breasts ached for the intimate contact of his body.

She wanted, Claire recognised dizzily, to press herself tightly against him, to rub her body against his as sinuously and sexily as a small cat; she wanted to feel the hard heat of his flesh against her own, the erotic rasp of his body hair against the nerve-shattering sensitivity of her desire-flooded breasts; she wanted...

She gave a small, shocked gasp of surprise as Brad suddenly bit her bottom lip erotically, his hands sliding down her arms to manacle her wrists as he lifted her arms gently above her head.

A thrill of pure, hot, womb-tightening sensation ran through her body in a powerful current as she sensed what he was going to do. The heat that flooded her lower body was at once fiercely and control-shatteringly new and yet somehow so familiar that she knew that it...that *he* was something her body and her emotions had secretly yearned for all her adult life.

She felt no sense of being constrained or afraid, no sense of discomfort or threat at the way he was holding her, only a hot, aching surge of sensual knowledge, an awareness of the deliberateness with which he moved. A tight, aching sensation of intense need made her eyes start to close in shivering appreciation of the way his mouth slowly caressed the sensitive flesh of her throat before moving downwards.

It seemed like an aeon before his mouth reached its first destination, before she was able to expel her pent-up breathing—a sharp, high cry of physical release as she felt him slowly and gently lapping the hard, swollen flesh of her nipple.

Unable to stop herself, Claire heard herself moan with pleasure, her whole body shuddering as Brad dropped her arms and gathered her close, her frantic response to him destroying his own self-control as his mouth, which had initially almost teased her with too gentle kisses, now suckled on her breasts with a fierce sensuality that made her move urgently with rhythmic longing against him, her body possessed of instincts and responses that she had never, ever imagined it might know or exhibit.

Brad's mouth moved with fierce urgency over her midriff and then her belly; his hands held her and stroked her and finally lowered her onto the bed, where not even the sight of him pushing away her robe as he knelt over her and slowly, with sensual deliberateness, slid his hands caressingly up over her parted thighs had the effect of making her feel self-conscious or apprehensive.

She could feel the faint tremor in his hands as he touched and held her, seeing the aching male hunger in his eyes as he lifted his head and looked deeply into her own before looking back at the soft, shadowed, exposed triangle of silky hair that not so much concealed her sex, Claire recognised as her heart started to race with feverish longing, but rather emphasised its feminine sensuality and allure.

She could see the way Brad's eyes darkened with open desire as he placed one hand over her, his fingertips stroking the silky hair, parting the softly fleshed lips which were already signalling their longing for his touch.

But as he knelt over her Claire's attention was suddenly caught by something. 'No, wait,' she demanded huskily.

'What is it?' he asked her. 'I won't hurt you, Claire. I won't do anything you don't want... I won't...'

Quickly she shook her head. 'No,' she whispered fiercely. 'It isn't...' Her fingers touched his wrist, marvelling at the strength of bone and sinew that his flesh covered. 'I want to see you...' she whispered huskily. 'I want to look... to watch...'

For a moment she thought that he didn't understand what she meant, but then, as his eyes met hers, she saw that he did, and her breath caught on a small, fierce stab of pleasure as she saw, too, how much her whispered plea had aroused him.

Silently she watched as he pushed aside the duvet, aware not only of the tautly male eroticism of his body but of the way he was trembling slightly as well, of the way he paused, hesitated almost nervously, as he watched her watching him.

That he should exhibit such nervousness filled her with female tenderness. Gently she reached out and touched him, running her fingertips from his breastbone right down to where the fine line of body hair became a silky male tangle, openly, thickly sexual, that cushioned the power and promise of what lay over it.

This was her first self-chosen intimate contact with male arousal, but somehow to Claire, as she slowly looked at Brad and absorbed the physical reality of him, it was as though a part of her had known him and known this for always.

Even before her fingertips ran slowly and exploratively along the length of his taut arousal she knew exactly how his whole body would stiffen and shudder beneath her touch... how he would moan softly beneath his breath and close his eyes, arching his spine as he submitted to her exploration, only the fierce rigidity with which the flesh she was touching swelled just that little bit more against her touch betraying how much it craved the pleasure of her caress.

A man's body was at once both so sexually powerful and dangerous and so vulnerable, Claire marvelled, watching Brad's jaw clench as he tried to control his reaction to her. If just this, her lightest touch, had the power to affect him so intensely, how would he react if she were to bend her head and press her lips to his tautly sensitive skin—to kiss and caress it, to slide...?

She gave a tiny gasp of shock when she heard Brad saying something savagely fierce under his breath as he removed her hand and then lowered his head over her body, kissing her stomach and then her thighs with a frenetic urgency, touching her, stroking and caressing her, first with his fingers and then with his mouth until she was turning and twisting beneath the unbearable pleasure of what he was doing to her, alternately shuddering with the seismic convulsions that engulfed her and pleading with him to stop, crying out to him that she couldn't endure such sensual ecstasy.

Only Brad wouldn't stop, and it wasn't until he was finally buried deep inside her, his body moving with rhythmic urgency within hers, his voice thick and guttural with praise and pleasure as he finally succumbed to his own desire, that she recognised that physical ecstasy and female fulfilment could be even more intense a second time than it had been the first.

Half an hour later, still feeling blissfully euphoric from the intensity of their lovemaking and emotionally dizzy from the unexpectedness of what had happened, Claire struggled to fight off the waves of sleep washing over her, murmuring a soft sound of appreciation as Brad drew her closer to his body and kept her there, unable, it seemed, to relinquish her, his lips feathering gently against her hair as Claire drifted off to sleep.

When she came awake abruptly later in the night, at first she had no idea where she was, but the physical sensation of Brad's hot body next to hers and the sound of his voice as he cried out something unintelligible in his sleep froze her into shocked awareness as she realised what she had done.

Her body shaking with reaction, she started to ease herself free of Brad's still constraining arm.

At some stage Brad must have switched off the lamp because the room was now almost in darkness. However, there was still enough light for Claire to be able to see that the fever which had originally brought her into Brad's room, anxious for his health, had disappeared. Still trembling, she eased herself out of his bed, her eyes widening as she caught sight of her discarded robe lying on the floor.

As she shrugged herself into it, her hands were trembling so much that she couldn't fasten the tie-belt.

Hot shame scorched her skin as she remembered how eagerly, how unbelievably provocatively she had silently encouraged Brad to remove it... As her mind relayed flickering, unwanted images of what had happened to her she shrank inwardly from what they were revealing to her. She didn't recognise the image of herself they were giving her, the message about herself that they were giving her. She didn't *want* to recognise them.

In her anxiety to get out of Brad's room she almost stumbled, holding her breath as he moved in his sleep, his forehead furrowing as he reached out an arm across the bed as though searching for her. For her...or merely for a woman...any woman...?

Had he known it was her when...when he had behaved in that incredibly sensual way, or had he simply been in the grip of some fevered state of semiconsciousness? Claire fervently prayed that it was the latter as she hurried back to her own bedroom.

But then, as she climbed into her cold bed, she stiffened. Brad had called her by her name... He had opened his eyes and looked at her, recognised her. He had whispered to her, made it clear that he wanted her.

How on earth was she ever going to be able to face him again? she wondered miserably. For a man to make love to a woman without being committed to her, without loving her, was still, in the eyes of a too cynical world, socially acceptable. For a woman to do the same thing...

But she had not done the same thing, had she? She...

Claire sat up in bed, hugging her arms around her knees, forcing herself to confront the truth.

She was not permitted the merciful excuse of being able to blame her behaviour on male hormones or a deep fever, and she knew that underneath the sheer sensuality of what she had done, the fierce intensity of a physical desire so strong that it had caught her off guard like an unexpectedly strong current in a previously placid stretch of calm water, she was emotionally drawn to Brad—emotionally responsive to him.

Emotionally drawn... A bitter sound of smothered hysterical laughter rasped at the back of her throat.

Be honest with yourself, she jeered inwardly; you're in love with him. You, a woman of your age, are making a fool of yourself with emotions more suited to a girl in her teens.

A woman of her age maybe, but she did not have the experience, the knowledge of herself as a sexual being, that other women of her age enjoyed, Claire admitted painfully. In that regard she *was* as naïve and unknowing as a girl in the throes of her first adolescent love affair. And her age made those feelings more painful, *more* hard to bear, not less.

'Admit it,' she whispered as she bent her aching head to her raised knees; 'you were attracted to him right from the start but you pretended not to know it, and tonight when he touched you...' She swallowed painfully.

She hadn't tried very hard to resist, to stop him, had she? On the contrary...

Why was it so hard for her to face the truth about her feelings for Brad?

Did she really need to ask herself that question?

Claire's mouth curled into a small, bitter expression of pain. No, of course she didn't. It was hard because she knew already the pain that loving Brad was going to cause her.

To love a man who didn't love you back when you were seventeen was bad enough, but at seventeen life still had the power to heal the hurts it inflicted. There would inevitably be another man, another love. But at thirty-four it was for ever, for life—a once-and-for-all love.

As Claire closed her eyes, willing the tears she could feel gathering at the back of her eyes not to fall, she reflected on how very little she actually seemed to have known about herself. All those years of believing that it would be impossible for her ever to share true physical intimacy with a man, all those years of believing that the trauma of her youth and the inhibitions, the doubts about her own sexuality... about herself...

Tonight had shown her just how wrong she had been. In Brad's arms, beneath Brad's touch, her body had flowered into the full bloom of its sensuality... of its sexuality.

What was going to happen when he woke up and remembered...? As Claire fought to suppress the pain that
she could feel seeping relentlessly through her body she
reflected that Irene was not going to be pleased when
she learned that Brad had moved out, which she knew
already was what was going to happen.

CHAPTER EIGHT

CLAIRE woke up with a start. She could hear the front doorbell ringing and the sun was streaming in through her uncurtained bedroom window. Groggily she lifted her head from her pillow and was appalled to discover that it was gone ten o'clock.

Throwing back the bedcovers, she reached for her robe, pulling it on over her naked body, avoiding looking at her reflection in the dressing-table mirror, her skin flushing slightly as the slow, almost voluptuous movements of her body silently betrayed the events of the previous evening.

As she hurried along the landing she saw that the door to Brad's bedroom stood open. The bed was empty and neatly made up. No need to ask herself why Brad had not woken her before he had left, she thought grimly.

Whoever was outside the front door was obviously getting impatient; a finger pressed the bell in a long, imperious ring.

As Claire went to open the door she could see through the glass panes a woman she didn't recognise standing outside with two small children—a young girl at her side and a baby in one arm.

When she pulled open the door to her she could see that the young woman was frowning anxiously and that she looked tired and drawn. The baby had started to cry and the girl joined in, the young mother closing her eyes in exasperation as she tried to calm them.

'Is Brad here?' she asked Claire anxiously, her frown returning as she appealed urgently, 'This is where he's staying, isn't it? He did give me the address but I wasn't sure I'd written it down properly.

'Yes... it's all right,' she soothed the baby, her soft, transatlantic accent so very similar to Brad's that just to hear it made Claire's susceptible heart turn over.

'Yes. You've got the right address,' she reassured the young woman, standing back to usher her inside and at the same time automatically offering to take the baby from her.

'Oh, yes... Thanks... He's very damp,' she informed Claire ruefully, 'and pretty hungry too...'

Claire wasn't really listening; her heart was turning over painfully inside her too tight chest as she looked into the baby's now fully opened eyes and saw just how like Brad's they were.

A spasm of deep, wrenching pain like nothing she had ever known seared through her, her eyes too dry for the tears she ached to cry, the small sound of protest she could feel rising in her throat luckily suppressed.

'I'm Brad's sister, by the way—Mary-Beth,' the young woman introduced herself as she ushered the little girl inside and then reached for their luggage.

His sister. As Claire focused on the other woman's back she could feel herself starting to tremble with relief. Just for a moment, looking at the baby and seeing Brad's eyes in his small and as yet not really fully formed face, she had thought... assumed...

'He is here, isn't he? I had to come. I had to see him,' she told Claire emotionally, her eyes suddenly filling with tears.

'No, I'm afraid he isn't,' Claire informed her. 'He'll probably be back soon, though,' she added comfortingly. 'I can give you the office number and you can ring him there,' she offered helpfully, but the other woman shook her head.

'No...no, I'd better wait until he gets back... You see, he...he doesn't...he isn't exactly expecting us...' She paced the hall edgily, avoiding Claire's eyes.

Something was very obviously wrong, Claire guessed. No one, however impetuous, came rushing across the Atlantic with two small children, one of them still too young to walk, just on a mere whim.

'You must be hungry and tired,' she said quietly. 'Let's go into the kitchen and see if we can find you something to eat, shall we?' she suggested softly to the baby, who had stopped crying but was gnawing hungrily on his fingers as he focused wonderingly on her unfamiliar face.

'I guess we are,' her unexpected visitor agreed, but Claire sensed that food was the last thing on her mind, and now that she had had the opportunity to study her a little more closely she could see the tell-tale signs of strain and unhappiness etched into her face and eyes. The little girl too, clinging so closely to her mother's side, had an expression in her eyes that had been caused by something more than the confusion of a long transatlantic journey.

Mary-Beth had said that she would wait for Brad to return, but Claire suspected that whatever had brought her rushing to find him meant that she needed to see her brother more urgently than that.

Her heart started to thud a little too fast at the thought of telephoning him. What would he think when he heard her voice? That because of last night she was making unfounded assumptions about him...about them...?

His sister's obvious need was more important than her own pride, Claire told herself firmly as she led the way to the kitchen, settling Mary-Beth in one of the comfortable Windsor chairs and then going to retrieve from the laundry room the high chair she kept for emergencies, still holding the baby, who was now quite contentedly gurgling up at her.

'You're obviously very good with children,' Mary-Beth told her ruefully, watching her. 'He's screamed practically the whole way here.'

'And he was sick three times,' a small voice piped up from Mary-Beth's side, the little girl's face stern with big-sisterly disapproval.

'This is Tara.' Mary-Beth introduced her daughter. 'And that smelly, damp bundle you're carrying is Abe junior...'

'Abe senior is my daddy,' Tara piped up. 'But he hasn't come with us. He's—'

'Hush now, Tara,' Mary-Beth interrupted quickly. 'I'm sorry,' she apologised to Claire. 'We're putting you to an awful lot of trouble. I should have rung Brad before we left but...'

Tears suddenly filled her eyes, and as she looked away Claire felt her own throat closing up in sympathy for her.

Half an hour later, when the children had both been fed and were soundly asleep upstairs in one of the bedrooms, Claire poured her unexpected visitor a fresh cup of coffee and tried again to persuade her to let her telephone Brad.

'No, no... Oh, where is he? I need to see him to talk to him. He's the only one...'

Fresh tears filled her eyes.

'When everything you thought you could rely on—everyone you thought you could rely on—lets you down and it seems that there's only one person left for you to turn to, you don't always think things through properly... Brad's always been more than just a brother to us. He's the one we always automatically turn to when things go wrong for us... and I guess that's why...'

She bit her lip and looked directly at Claire as she went on huskily, 'You've probably already worked out why I'm here... I found out three days ago that Abe, my husband, has been having an affair with a girl at work.

'He tried to deny it, of course, but they were seen downtown in a bar by a close friend of mine. He told me that he had to work late... and I believed him, even though I knew she'd been making a play for him. I thought he loved me, you see,' she said sadly.

'Look, you've had a long flight. Why don't you go upstairs and lie down?' Claire suggested gently. She could see from the deep unhappiness in the other woman's eyes just how much her husband's infidelity had hurt her.

'Abe kept insisting that it wasn't true—that he was simply trying to help the girl sort out her personal problems. He said he hadn't told me because he knew the way I'd react... He said that I never had time to listen to him any more anyway, because the children were more important to me than he was. He even said that Brad mattered more to me than him... that I paid more attention to what Brad had to say... that it was Brad I always turned to for help...'

As her emotions caught up with her she swallowed painfully and then said huskily, 'I think I will go up and have a rest, if you don't mind. I'm beginning to feel that so much has happened that I can't even think straight any more...Abe doesn't even know I'm here,' she added tiredly. 'I just wanted to see Brad so much... I needed him so much... I just kinda grabbed the kids and some stuff and phoned the airline and the next thing I knew we were all on our way...'

As she stood up she stifled a yawn, her eyes dark with exhaustion.

*   *   *

Claire waited until she was sure that Mary-Beth was asleep before telephoning the office.

Brad, she discovered, wasn't there and so she spoke to Tim instead, who informed her that Brad was expected back within the hour.

'Could you ask him to give me a ring as soon as he comes back?' Claire asked her brother-in-law, without explaining why she needed to speak to him. Brad's family was his private affair and she didn't think it right to discuss what had happened with anyone else.

A quick check upstairs confirmed that her visitors were all still asleep.

As she put fresh towels in the bathroom she wondered how long they were likely to stay, and also wondered, half-enviously, what it must be like to have someone like Brad to turn to—someone you could rely on so completely that you could simply walk out of your home with two children and a couple of suitcases, knowing that if you could get to him he would solve your problems for you.

She was being a little unfair, Claire reproved herself. No amount of brotherly concern could surely compensate for an unfaithful husband and a broken marriage. And she had seen the apprehension and confusion in little Tara's eyes. An uncle, no matter how loving and concerned, could not replace a father.

Not that she blamed Mary-Beth for feeling as she did. To discover that your husband—the man you love and to whom you had committed yourself and who you believed had committed himself to you, the father of your children—had been seeing another woman...had been making love with her...must be one of the most painful experiences that life could hold.

As she went back downstairs Claire checked her fridge. From the way Mary-Beth had toyed with the food she had had earlier Claire doubted that she would have much appetite, but the children were a different matter, especially the baby.

She had plenty of fresh vegetables and fruit that she could cook for him and put through the blender, Claire decided, and as for Tara—well, with a bit of luck the little girl might be enticed into helping her, which would give her mother the chance to have some private conversation with Brad.

Claire suspected from the anxious looks that Tara had given her mother when her father had been mentioned that the little girl was already aware that something was wrong between her parents.

Children, even very young ones, were dismayingly quick to pick up on things like that and to suffer through it, Claire knew, often blaming themselves for the problems between their mothers and fathers.

A small sound from upstairs checked her and she paused to listen to it... Was it the baby crying?

As she went towards the door she heard the sound of a car pulling up outside.

Brad? She had expected him to telephone her, not to come straight back. A small flutter of apprehension gripped her stomach.

This would be the first time they had seen one another since last night—the first time since... But this was not the time for her to become involved in her own feelings; she...

She tensed as the kitchen door opened and Brad came striding in. When he saw her anxious expression his forehead creased in a frown and he hurried towards her.

'Claire, what is it? What's wrong?' he asked, starting to reach for her as though he was going to take her in his arms, Claire recognised, her throat tight with emotion, her colour starting to rise self-consciously as she fought the temptation to move closer to him, her body already reacting to his presence, his proximity, to its need to recreate the intimacy they had shared last night, its need to encourage the physical bond it wanted to establish between them.

Claire acknowledged how easy it would be simply to close the distance between them, to walk into his arms as though it was her right to do so.

Against her will she found herself looking at his mouth, her glance lingering on it betrayingly as she felt her own lips start to tremble slightly. Last night's intimacy had left her so sensually, so sensitively attuned to him that she could almost feel the warm pleasure of his mouth on hers.

'Claire...'

The hoarse urgency with which he said her name brought her back to reality, her body tensing as she heard sounds from the hall.

'Brad—' she began warningly, but the door was already opening and Mary-Beth was rushing into her brother's arms, crying emotionally,

'Oh, Brad, thank the Lord you're here...'

'Mary-Beth...?' Claire could hear the surprise in Brad's voice as he held his sister and looked questioningly at Claire over her head. 'What...?'

Quietly Claire left the room and closed the door behind her. They would have things to say to one another that needed to be said in private, without her.

She could hear the baby starting to cry and moved instinctively towards the stairs to go and comfort him.

When she went into the bedroom Tara had obviously just woken up.

'Where's my mommy?' she asked Claire uncertainly.

'She's downstairs talking to your uncle Brad,' Claire told her, and then asked, 'Do you know where the spare nappies are? I think your brother needs changing.'

'Nappies?' The little girl's face creased in confusion whilst Claire quickly tried to recall the American word for what she wanted.

'Diapers,' she remembered with relief, then gently but firmly involved Tara in the job of cleaning and changing her small brother, deliberately drawing it out as long as she could to give Mary-Beth a chance to talk to Brad. Claire suspected that she would not want Tara to overhear what she had to say to Brad about her husband's infidelity. The little girl was obviously already distressed enough by what was happening.

As Claire picked up the now dry and cooing little boy to give him a cuddle she saw the way Tara kept glancing anxiously towards the door and guessed that she wouldn't be able to keep her distracted for very much longer.

To her relief she heard the kitchen door opening and Mary-Beth's and Brad's voices on the stairs.

'Mommy,' Tara demanded as soon as her mother came into the bedroom, 'when are we going home? I want my daddy...'

Mary-Beth had obviously been crying and Tara's mouth started to tremble ominously as she looked at her mother. It was Brad who saved the situation, following his sister into the room and swinging the little girl up into his arms, saying cheerfully, 'Hello, pumpkin...'

'Uncle Brad... Uncle Brad...' Tara squealed in obvious pleasure, hugging him tightly round the neck.

'I'll get on to the airport and see how quickly they can get you a return flight,' Brad was saying to Mary-Beth over Tara's head.

'I'm not going back—not on my own, not without you,' Mary-Beth insisted.

'Mary-Beth, I've already explained why I can't come with you,' Brad told her firmly. 'I have commitments here.'

'Maybe, but they aren't as important as your commitment to your family; they can't be, Brad,' Mary-Beth told him quickly. 'You know the uncles will understand. I need you.'

Claire could see that Brad was frowning.

'Mary-Beth, I can't.'

'Then I'm not going back,' she told him determinedly. 'Not on my own.'

'Abe—' Brad began, but Mary-Beth refused to listen.

'I don't want to talk about him, or *to* him.'

'You *have* to talk,' Brad told her quietly. 'For the kids' sake, if nothing else. He is still their father and he does have certain rights—'

'He has no rights. He lost those the day he started fooling around with that—that...' Mary-Beth had started to protest bitterly but Brad shook his head warningly as Tara looked at her mother in anxious concern. 'If you want me to talk to him then you're going to have to be there too,' Mary-Beth insisted.

Claire could see that Brad wasn't too pleased about his sister's demands.

'There's no way I want to so much as see him again after what he's done...' she announced.

It was plain to Claire that Brad's sister's temperament was as tempestuous and fiery as her dark red hair suggested, and there was no doubt also that she was deeply hurt by her husband's infidelity. Beneath her very obvious anger Claire could see the misery and pain in her eyes.

'You said Abe denied being involved with anyone else,' Brad was reminding her. 'He said—'

'He would say that, wouldn't he?' Mary-Beth derided bitterly. 'He knows what he stands to lose. Oh, Brad, how could he... I thought he loved me...us...'

Tears welled up in her eyes and Tara, seeing her mother's distress, started to cry noisily in sympathy.

'Would you like me to take the children?' Claire offered quickly. 'You must both still have things you need to discuss...'

'I've said everything I want to say,' Mary-Beth said fiercely. 'I don't care what you say, Brad; there's no way I'm going back to him and I didn't come all the way over here to have you make me...or to listen to you defending what he's done. I thought you'd be more understanding...more sympathetic...'

She was crying in earnest now. Quietly Claire held out her arms to Tara, trying not to let the revealing flush of pleasure she could feel heating the pit of her stomach flood betrayingly into her face when Brad smiled at her with appreciative relief as he handed his niece over to her.

'I want to stay with my mommy...' Tara started to protest as Claire took hold of her, but Claire had enough experience from her work at the school to know how to deal with her apprehensive need to remain with her mother.

'Do you?' she said calmly. 'Oh, dear. I was hoping you'd come downstairs with me and help me make some special bis...er...cookies. I expect you're very good at baking, aren't you?' she asked.

'Yes. I'm very good,' Tara agreed, and then asked, 'What kind of cookies?'

'What kind would you like to make?' Claire asked her. The baby had gone peacefully back to sleep, she noticed as she gently shepherded Tara out of the room.

She and Tara had almost finished their cookie-baking exercise before Mary-Beth and Brad reappeared, and during the half-hour or so that they had been together

Claire had learned a good deal about her Mommy and Daddy and how much she loved them both from Tara, who had chattered happily to her as they worked together.

'It looks like I'm going to have to go back to the States with Mary-Beth. I've managed to get us seats on a flight this evening,' Brad told Claire tersely as he obeyed Tara's demand that he come and see what she had been making.

'I'm sorry about all this...' he added grimly, making a small gesture that included his sister and Tara.

'It's all right,' Claire assured him. 'I'm just glad that you were able to respond so quickly to my message. I hadn't expected you to come straight back—'

'What message?' Brad asked her, frowning.

Claire stared at him.

'I rang the office to tell you about Mary-Beth, and when you weren't there I left a message with Tim for you to ring me.'

If he hadn't got her message then how had he known to come back? Claire wondered. But before she could say anything Mary-Beth was demanding his attention, wanting to know exactly what time their flight was and worrying about the fact that she had neglected to bring enough baby food for Abe junior with her.

'You should have thought about that before you left,' Brad told her sharply.

Whilst he was obviously making every attempt to sort out his sister's problems for her, he did not appear to be as sympathetic to her plight as Claire had expected him to be, and was certainly nothing like as partisan, refusing to join Mary-Beth in condemning her husband and rather to the contrary suggesting to her that she should have discussed the situation more fully with Abe before walking out and subjecting her two small children to all the stress and bewilderment of a transatlantic flight.

Sensing that Mary-Beth was unhappy with her brother's response, Claire quickly offered to take her to the local supermarket where she would be able to buy some branded baby food for her little boy.

'Brad, could you take me?' Mary-Beth appealed. 'I just can't think straight at the moment.'

It was only natural that Mary-Beth should want her brother with her rather than a stranger, Claire told herself firmly, and it was no doubt illogical of her to feel, on the strength of what little they had actually shared, so emotionally bereft and excluded from what was going on.

Several times since he had returned to the house Brad had looked as if he wanted to say something to her, Claire acknowledged, and it was obvious that he was none too pleased with his sister's disruption of his life. But, in reality, what else could he do other than agree to her demands that he return home with her? Claire acknowledged.

It was plain to her, even without knowing Mary-Beth or having met her husband, that it would need all of Brad's skilled counsel and wisdom to heal the rift in his sister's marriage.

'Claire,' she heard him saying quietly, his hand touching her arm lightly, as though he wanted to draw her away from Mary-Beth and the children. As though... as though... *what*? Claire asked herself ruefully. As though he wanted to isolate both of them from his family, as though he wanted to have *her* to himself. That's some imagination you've got there, she warned herself.

'I really am sorry,' he told her in a low voice. 'If I thought there was any way I could persuade Mary-Beth to go home on her own—'

'She needs you, Brad,' Claire interrupted him gently. And so do I, her heart cried silently, but of course she couldn't allow herself to voice such words and wouldn't have done no matter what the circumstances; to have done so would have been immature and selfish. 'She's obviously very upset about...about her husband,' Claire felt bound to add.

'Yes.' Brad looked rather grim. 'She always has a tendency to flare up over nothing and I doubt that this will be any exception. Abe's just not the type to stray from his marriage.'

'Mary-Beth obviously doesn't share that view,' Claire pointed out wryly.

'No,' Brad agreed heavily, glancing at his sister, who was trying to soothe the children's fretting. 'This couldn't have happened at a worse time...' he began to say; his hand was still resting on her arm but now the light grip of his fingers had somehow or other become a gentle stroke.

An automatic reflex action to the feel of her skin beneath them or the tender, soundless reassurance of a lover? Claire wasn't sure.

'Brad,' Mary-Beth called out impatiently, 'you're going to have to get to that supermarket.'

Was she imagining the regret she could see in Brad's eyes as he released her arm and moved away from her? Claire wondered.

'And so Brad's gone back to America with his sister?' Hannah asked as Claire started to unload her dishwasher.

'Yes, that's right,' Claire agreed woodenly.

Hannah had come round half an hour ago, two hours after Brad and Mary-Beth had left with the children. By now, no doubt, they would be airborne and on their way back home.

'I'm not sure when I'll be coming back but it should be within the week,' Brad had told her before he'd left. They had been standing in the hall, Brad frowning down at her, his expression grimly sombre—because he was concerned about his sister or because he was regretting what had happened between them the previous night? Claire had wondered.

She flinched now as she recalled her own brief moment of weakness when she had almost reached out to him and begged him to...

To what? To tell her that their lovemaking had been as earth-shaking, as cataclysmically, emotionally and physically intense for him as it had been for her? That, like her, he had been confronted by a revelation of emotions for her—love for her so strong that he knew his life would never be the same again?

Fortunately, she had been able to stop herself before she had done anything more than stretch out her hand towards him.

Mary-Beth had hugged her warmly before she'd left, thanking her appreciatively for all that she had done, but Brad hadn't made any move to touch her, Claire had noticed.

'How long will he be gone for?' Hannah pressed. 'You're going to miss him. There's something about having a man about the house...'

'He's only been here a couple of days, Hannah,' Claire reminded her neighbour tersely, and was instantly ashamed of herself when she saw the hurt expression in Hannah's eyes. The trouble was that Hannah was right—or almost...

It wasn't just a matter of her *going* to miss Brad, she was already doing so—missing him, aching for him, yearning for him, filled with all manner of insecurities and doubts, wondering if as far as he was concerned his sister's marital difficulties had occurred most opportunely—contrary to what he had said before he'd left. It was a galling thought and an extremely painful one.

So you went to bed with him and had sex, Claire taunted herself later when Hannah was gone. So what? Why should that have had any deep meaning for him?

Did Brad even remember what had happened between them? she pondered starkly. He had, after all, been in the grip of an extremely strong fever earlier in the evening.

Which was the worst scenario for her? she wondered painfully. For him not to have remembered a single thing about them being together, or for him to have remembered but to have decided that it was something that he simply felt had no real meaning for him?

And, given the choice, which would she have preferred—to have experienced all that she had in his arms, to have discovered her capacity for emotional and physical love and endure all the pain that must surely now follow, or to have remained in celibate obliviousness?

It was a question she didn't feel she could answer, not with all the long, empty nights ahead of her without Brad beside her.

CHAPTER NINE

A WEEK went by without Claire hearing anything from Brad, and then another, and then halfway through the third she received a telephone call from Tim advising her that Brad had been in touch with him.

'He did try to ring you but he said there was no reply. His uncle—the one who runs the business—has had a heart attack and is in Intensive Care and Brad has had to step in and take over from him, so obviously there's no question of him returning here in the immediate future.'

'But what about his things? They're still here,' Claire protested. Her body felt numb with shock; until she'd heard Tim telling her that Brad wouldn't be coming back she hadn't realised how much she had been depending on him returning . . . how strongly she had been clinging to that frail link between them.

Now Tim had severed it, leaving her feeling that she was crashing through space, tumbling helplessly from a great height, her stomach seized with fear and nausea as her whole world dissolved around her.

'I expect he'll want us to make arrangements to ship whatever he's left behind out to him,' Tim told her. 'Just let me know what there is and we can sort all that out for you.'

After she had replaced the receiver Claire went upstairs, moving like a sleepwalker as she went into the room that Brad had occupied. Was she imagining it or did the very air in there still carry a faint scent of him—

of his soap, his skin, himself? Her whole body bowed with misery and loss.

She went across to the bed, smoothing her fingertips over the pillow, hot tears filling her eyes.

It was ridiculous for her to be behaving in this fashion, she derided herself. She was a grown woman. Grown women didn't fall intensely and passionately in love in the space of a handful of days—or at least they weren't supposed to. Their hearts weren't supposed to ache with all the intensity and anguish with which hers was aching right now, and nor were their bodies.

Their bodies...her body... Her body. Oh, how it had deceived her, led her into a trap of false security, letting her believe that it was impossible for it to feel, to want, to *need* the way it was doing right now.

Brad had said that he'd tried to ring her, Tim had told her. Her head dipped defensively as she remembered those last, frantic hours before he had left, his sister's resentment at what she had seen as Brad's support of her husband in his insistence that she needed to return home to talk to him and that it wasn't fair on her children—on their children—simply to walk out, no matter what provocation she might think she personally had had to do so.

Brad had tried to talk privately to her then and foolishly she had hoped that he had wanted to reassure her, to offer her if not his love then at least the reassurance that there was something between them worth pursuing. But now she wondered if she might have been wrong, if what he had wanted to say to her was more along the lines of Thank you, it was very nice, but now it's over.

Over... Her throat constricted on a small half-sob, a painful spasm of emotion. It had never really properly begun. What was there, in reality, to be over? All they had had, all there had been was simply a...a one-night stand . . . a bit of a sexual adventure, and she had been a fool to believe that it was anything more.

And, that being the case, there was precious little point in compounding her folly by thinking about what might have been, tormenting herself with implausible, unrealistic daydreams. No, she would be better off simply forgetting about the whole incident . . . about Brad himself— forgetting it and firmly locking the door on it and throwing away the key.

It was an easy enough resolve to make, but a much harder one to keep, Claire discovered in the weeks that followed.

Irene commented in a slightly miffed manner on her lacklustre response to life in general and to her own good news in particular that Tim had responded so positively to Brad's suggestions, including his recommendation that Tim should consider going on a self-assertion training course.

'Of course it will mean that someone will have to come over from America to take charge of things for a while,' Irene had confided. 'But Brad says he has someone in mind for that—their top distributor over there. Tim is already in contact with him and they seem to be getting on very well.'

But even her sister-in-law's plans for the future failed to move Claire to anything more than dull indifference—a reaction which she herself felt barely registered as a meagre one out of ten on the scale of her emotional misery, but which apparently Irene had seen fit to accord a much higher anxiety-rating, as Claire discovered when she received an unscheduled visit from her stepdaughter in the middle of what had so far been a particularly harrowing day.

She had discovered earlier in the morning that the school where she worked was to be closed, its pupils amalgamated with those at another school on the other side of town.

It wasn't so much the fact that her voluntary services would no longer be required that upset her but the knowledge of how difficult some of their children would find it to adapt to new and, to them, potentially threatening surroundings and routines, and she was still worrying about the fate of the children when Sally arrived unexpectedly.

'Is something wrong?' Claire asked her stepdaughter anxiously, knowing that she should have been at work.

'According to Aunt Irene *I'm* the one who should be asking *you* that question,' Sally told her forthrightly, adding more gently, 'I haven't wanted to pry, but it's been obvious ever since we got back from honeymoon that something is wrong. Every time I've spoken to you it's been almost as though you're not really... You've been so... so distant almost that I had begun...' Sally paused and bit her lip, her face flushing slightly.

'It isn't anything to do with the wedding, is it... and with that trick Chris and I played on the three of you with the wedding bouquet? Only when I rang Star the other day she was very curt with me and said she was too busy to speak to me, and as for Poppy—well, I know how she's always felt about Chris, but she was so young when she first developed her crush on him.

'I never meant to hurt any of you,' Sally told her urgently, coming over to kneel down beside Claire and to lay her head on her lap as she had done when she was a little girl in need either of a confessional for some minor crime or some extra cosseting and reassurance.

Automatically Claire reached out to stroke the shining head of hair just as she had done so many times when Sally had been growing up.

'If you're cross with me about the bouquet, please believe me, we...I only did it because—well, because Chris and I... Well, I'm so happy myself, I just wanted all of you—but most especially you...'

Sally bit her lip, her voice slightly strained as she continued emotionally, 'You've been...you are such a wonderful mother to me, much better than...a much better parent to me than Dad ever was. I've always known that and, well...I've always loved you...more...best...but it wasn't until Chris pointed it out to me that I realised that your marriage, that my father...'

She raised her head and looked at Claire. 'It must have been very difficult for you. After all, he never made any secret of the fact that Paula...that...'

'He still loved your mother,' Claire supplied for her. 'She was *your* mother, Sally,' she reminded her stepdaughter gently, 'and I honestly don't mind you referring to her as that... You see, I *know* I have my own place in your love and in your life, and if anything it isn't jealousy or envy I feel for her, but sadness and pity because she was deprived of so much pleasure in not being here to watch you growing up.

'When you have children of your own they're going to want to know about her and you're going to want to tell them, but *I* shall be the one who cuddles them and tells them stories and gives them forbidden treats...'

'You'll always be Mum to me,' Sally told her tearfully. 'Always... I know there's been a bit of gossip about the bouquet and the pact the three of you made not to get married because of it—Hannah told me and I've heard it from someone else as well—but I honestly never meant to cause any of you any embarrassment or to hurt you...

'I know that, Sally,' Claire reassured her.

'Well, if that's not what's wrong, then what is it?' Sally persisted. 'And don't tell me "nothing", because it's obvious that something is wrong.'

'I heard this morning that they're going to close the school,' Claire told her.

'Oh, no. I am sorry... I know how much you've enjoyed working there.' She stood up, her face and voice lightening with relief as she added, 'Irene was convinced that the reason you've been so withdrawn has something to do with that American you had staying with you. Bart—'

'Brad,' Claire corrected her quietly, getting up to go and fill the kettle to make them both a hot drink and keeping her face carefully averted just in case something in her expression should betray her.

Just saying Brad's name had made her heart somersault violently and it was now thudding so heavily against her chest wall that it was practically making her dizzy and slightly faint.

For the first time ever Claire actually felt glad when her stepdaughter had gone. Right now Sally was still living in a cloud of post-honeymoon euphoric bliss, but once that started to fade and she was back to being her normal sharp-eyed self Claire doubted that she would be able to keep the truth from her for very long. If *Irene* had already guessed that something was wrong—and, even worse, why—what chance did she have of concealing the truth from Sally?

The answer lay in her own hands, Claire told herself firmly. If she didn't want the pain and humiliation of her nearest and dearest discovering how stupid she had been, then she was going to have to make much more of an effort to force herself to forget Brad and her love for him.

More of an effort. She gave a small, twisted smile. Right now simply getting through the day without him was just about as much effort as she was capable of making, which was pathetic and ridiculous given the fact that she had only known him a matter of days.

Maybe in that short space of time she had developed an emotional rapport with him, an emotional intimacy which had led to her telling him things about herself that she had never dreamed of confiding to anyone else. Maybe during that time she had developed an emotional need for him, an emotional hunger and intensity... which he quite plainly had not reciprocated, she reminded herself flatly. If he had...

As she cleared away her and Sally's dirty coffee-mugs she paused to stare blindly out of her kitchen window. Next week it would be three months since the wedding. She had put a red cross by the date on her kitchen wall-calendar.

As she glanced desolately at it she reflected grimly that at least she of the trio who had fallen into Sally's carefully orchestrated trap would be able to keep their rendezvous knowing that there was no chance of her breaking the light-hearted vow they had all made to remain single.

Quietly Brad watched from the sidelines as his family busied themselves with their self-appointed tasks.

Today they were holding their annual barbecue—an event that Brad himself had instituted the year after their parents' death, when, instead of grieving and mourning their loss in the traditional way, for the sake of the younger siblings and to ensure that their parents were never forgotten he had decided to hold a small barbecue to celebrate the fact that *they* were still together, that their parents *had* loved them and still loved them, even if they could not be there with them to show it.

Over the years the original small, homely event had expanded until it was now almost a local institution, with virtually the whole town seeming to attend, its venue having moved from the backyard of their home to a site on the lake shore.

Spring was just beginning to give way to summer and the days were longer and warmer. Later in the year this tree-sheltered site would be enervatingly stifling, but right now it was just protectively warm enough for the younger members of the group to beg pleadingly to be allowed into the water.

Brad smiled ruefully to himself, witnessing the clumsy, unpractised flirtation that one of his nephews was attempting with a disdainful redhead who one day was going to be stunningly attractive but who right now still wore her hair in braids and had a sexually pre-adolescent, thin, leggy body.

Once it had hurt him almost unbearably, knowing that his parents had died at this time of the year when nature was so full of promise and vigour, when everything was green and fresh and growing, but over the years that pain had softened into acceptance.

'You look very pensive.'

Brad smiled as Mary-Beth came over to him, slipping her arm through his and resting her head on his shoulder.

'I still haven't thanked you properly for insisting that I come back and talk properly to Abe. If I hadn't done...' She gave a small, rueful shake of her head. 'That temper of mine; you'd have thought by now I'd have learnt not to trust it.'

'I'd have thought by now you *would* have learnt to trust Abe,' Brad told her dryly.

'Well, you know how it is... Somehow, losing Mom and Dad... I guess I'm always going to feel a bit insecure...like thinking that Abe was having an affair when he was doing no such thing. But you're not much better,' she accused her brother. 'Look at the way you've stayed single...avoided any emotional commitment.'

Avoided emotional commitment. Brad frowned as he looked back at her. 'And how the hell do you work that one out?' he demanded grimly. 'Look around you, Mary-Beth, and tell me that again.'

'Oh, I don't mean you've avoided any emotional commitment to us,' Mary-Beth protested. 'You've been the best brother...the very best there could ever be. But...haven't you ever wanted anyone of your own, Brad? I mean we've all married... Don't you feel lonely sometimes, wish that you'd...?' She bit her lip as she saw the way that he was looking at her.

'Now don't you go putting that stern elder-brother look on your face with me. We all know how much you've sacrificed for us, how much you must curse us all to perdition at times, especially the uncles...'

She paused, drawing an abstract pattern in the sandy earth with the toe of her shoe. 'We all know you didn't want to go to Britain...nor to come back and take over the business. And *I* know, even if the others don't, that the old boat you've got down at the jetty is your equivalent of what us kids used to call our "running-away money". But if you really left here to sail around the world on your own, Brad, you'd hate it. You're a family man...a patriarch—'

'Don't bet money on it,' Brad advised her harshly, preparing to walk away, but Mary-Beth tugged on his arms, restraining him.

'Don't go yet; there's something else I wanted to say. We all know that Uncle Joe wouldn't have survived his heart attack if you hadn't come back...if you hadn't been in there pitching for him, but he's never going to be strong enough to go back to running the business, Brad, and we—'

'You what?' he asked her grimly. 'You've been deputised to soften me up and make sure I won't get any ideas about wanting to lead my own life, is that it?'

'Brad...'

Brad knew how much he'd upset her and cursed himself under his breath as he saw the tears in her eyes.

'You've changed so much recently,' Mary-Beth accused him. 'Become so withdrawn...so...so angry. All we want is for you to be happy.'

Later on, after they'd hugged and made up, Brad watched as she walked to join her husband and children.

Everyone here bar him had someone of their own, he reflected bleakly. Once that would not have bothered him; once he would not even have had such a thought, because *they* were *all* his family—a part of him, as he was of them; once he would never have spent an event like this standing on the sidelines wishing with all his heart that he were somewhere else, and with someone else.

Why hadn't Claire returned his phone call? He had tried so hard to make time to talk properly, privately with her before he and Mary-Beth had left, but the opportunity had just not been there. And then arriving home to be greeted by the news that his uncle Joe was seriously ill and was not expected to survive had meant that his own personal emotional needs and desires had had to be pushed to one side whilst he dealt with the practical problems that his uncle's heart attack had caused.

When he had finally got the time to himself to ring her she hadn't been there and he had had to speak to

Tim instead to explain what had happened. All week he had expected Claire to ring, rushing home whenever he could to check his answering machine.

But when one week had gone by and then another without her getting in touch he had told himself that he already had the answer to the question that he had secretly wanted to ask her, and that there was no point in going over and over in his mind... in his body those precious, gut-wrenching hours that they had spent together as lovers, that special, heart-aching time when he had hoped... believed... when he had finally recognised that he had at last found the thing—the person— that he had subconsciously been looking for all his adult life, and that without her in it his life would go on being incomplete.

He would go on being incomplete. This... *she* was the reason for all the dissatisfaction he had felt with his life over the years; *she* was the reason she had never felt able to reach out to any other woman in a way that would make her a permanent part of his life.

Was it his fault that she did not feel the same way? *Had* he rushed her... frightened her... put her off with his inability to control his sexual desire for her? Knowing what he did about her past, shouldn't he have been able to take things more slowly, to let her set the pace for any physical intimacy between them?

But it hadn't been any chauvinistic male need to prove either to her or himself that he possessed some magical ability to restore her sexuality to her, to reactivate it, that had motivated him; he knew that. He had simply wanted her so much... been so overwhelmed by his love for her that the sad, pathetic truth was that he had been totally unable to stop himself.

What kind of admission was that from a grown man... a mature man to have to make? he wondered in dry self-disgust. And he was *surprised* because Claire didn't want anything more to do with him?

On the other side of the clearing his uncle Joe, still restricted to a wheelchair but very much back in control of his life, beckoned to him. Warily Brad crossed the clearing and crouched down beside his uncle's wheelchair, asking him with a cheerfulness he didn't feel, 'How do you think it's going, Joe? Seems like everyone is having a good time.'

'Everyone but you,' his uncle told him forthrightly. 'No, don't bother denying it,' he added before Brad could speak. 'I've been watching you this past half-hour and it seems to me...' He paused and then said shrewdly, 'Seems to me you haven't been the same since you came back from England.'

'Much you would know,' Brad scoffed banteringly. 'When I came back from England you were in Intensive Care, giving us all the fright of our lives.'

'Well, I've made my three score and ten—and some besides,' Joe reminded him virtuously, but Brad wasn't deceived. He knew his uncle and his soft-spoken determination to live to celebrate his one hundredth birthday.

'You're an old fraud,' he told Joe ruefully now.

'And you're a fool,' the older man came back, watching him with fierce fondness. 'None can deny that you've done a good job standing in for your parents, Brad, nor that you've always put others before yourself, but they're all grown and gone now and unless you want to end up lonesome and alone...

'Who is she?' he asked craftily. 'Someone you met in England...? I was stationed over there during the war, you know; nearly married an English girl myself... My, but they're pretty. Would have married her, too, if she hadn't decided she preferred a fighter pilot to me. Worse mistake I ever made.'

Brad gave his uncle a frowning look. Joe, as he knew from wide experience, was a shameless manipulator of the truth when it suited him and this was certainly the first that he had ever heard of a wartime romance. His uncle's shrewdness in guessing about Claire had thrown him off guard, though.

'I've never heard about any English girl before,' he told his uncle.

'That's because I don't mention her. Don't like to admit to having made a mistake. That's a trait we both share... Should have married her when I had the chance, only I thought I'd kinda make her wait a little. I was young and I dare say a little swelled-headed at times. She didn't want to wait, though, and I lost her...

'Oh, I got over it... kinda... I came home after the war, met your aunt Grace and we got married, but I never forgot my English girl. Margaret, her name was. Peggy, they called her. Pretty as a rose, she was, with the softest skin.' He gave a sentimental sigh.

'Oh, Grace and I got on well enough together. She'd lost a fiancé during the war herself and so we both knew the score. Kinda makes you think, though. When I look around me now, see all of you together... If I'd married Peggy perhaps *my* grandchildren would be here now. There's nothing like having a family of your own, Brad.'

'I *have* a family,' Brad pointed out brusquely to him. And besides, she... my English girl... doesn't want me, he wanted to say, but the habit of keeping his own problems to himself, which had begun with his parents' death, was too deeply ingrained now to be overcome.

'A man belongs where his heart is, Brad; that's his true home,' his uncle told him quietly.

His uncle was right, Brad acknowledged later as the first of the early-evening shadows started to fall and the family gathered around the fire, the little ones snuggling up to their parents, the older ones—the soon-to-be teenagers—hanging together in their own small, private group, too old now to want to mimic those they saw as the babies of the family by staying with their parents and still too young to be allowed to separate themselves from the family group.

Abe picked up his guitar; he was a good musician, with a tuneful voice. When Mary-Beth had first met him he had been the lead singer in a local group; Brad smiled to himself, remembering how he had come the stern, heavy older brother, warning her about getting involved with a boy who played in a band.

Abe started to sing an old folk tune familiar to all of them; the other adults joined in, their voices gradually swelled by those of the youngsters, the unlikely mingling of all their voices producing a surprisingly harmonious sound—rather like the mingling of the family itself, Brad reflected. But for him a vitally important note was missing—a vitally needed sweetness, a vitally important person.

Quietly he turned away from the fire.

On the other side of the lake his boat still waited for those all-important repairs, but his dream of sailing her had lost its savour. His life felt empty... *he* felt empty, he recognised.

His uncle had been right. His heart wasn't here any longer; it was thousands of miles away across the Atlantic with a woman whose soft cries of love still returned at night, every night, to haunt and torment him.

Claire... Claire...

CHAPTER TEN

SHE was obviously the first to arrive for their lunch rendezvous, Claire recognised as the head waiter escorted her through the almost empty restaurant and into the conservatory, seating her at a central table with a wonderful view of the hotel gardens with such a flourish that she felt it was a shame that there was no one else there to witness it.

Giving him a warm smile as a reward for his professionalism and a compensation for his lack of a worthy audience for it, she refused his offer of an aperitif.

If she hadn't spoken to the other two earlier in the week to confirm their arrangement she would have been tempted to think that they weren't coming.

Her heart had gone out to Poppy when she had telephoned her and heard her subdued voice.

'The most peculiar thing has happened,' Sally had told her importantly the day prior to her telephone call. 'Chris has forbidden me, on pain of total withdrawal of my chocolate-bar allowance, to talk about it, but...'

'But...?' Claire had pressed, but Sally had shaken her head regretfully.

'I can't tell you, but if it is true I just can't believe... Although Chris says he always thought that...'

'Poppy's fallen in love with someone else?' Claire had suggested helpfully.

'Well...no...no...' Sally had shaken her head firmly. 'I promised Chris I wouldn't say anything. It's all a bit delicate, you see...a bit...well, a bit difficult...and,

169

to be honest, I'm still not sure I believe...' She had given Claire an apologetic look. 'I want to tell you but...'

'It's all right,' Claire had comforted her. 'Poppy is in a very vulnerable position at the moment,' she had added gently, inwardly reflecting on how much she would hate it if she thought that people were gossiping, speculating about her relationship with Brad, especially since the semi-public knowledge of their jokingly made vow of celibacy seemed to have added a certain piquancy to any gossip about their love lives. 'Obviously Chris wants to protect her from any additional hurt; that's only natural.'

'Yes, it is,' Sally had agreed, giving her a grateful hug. 'You will let me know if there are any signs of cracks appearing in the walls of female single solidarity, though, won't you?' she had added more light-heartedly.

'Certainly not,' Claire had told her roundly. 'It's one for all and all for one and you're the *last* person I would tell,' she had added teasingly.

'Mmm...well, I haven't heard anything from Star,' Sally had continued, 'in simply ages. I know she's been away a lot. Did you know, by the way, that Uncle Tim has consulted her about a new PR image for the company? Aunt Irene told me.'

Claire had made a noncommittal response, only too well aware of the fact that she had been avoiding Irene and all too well aware of how easily her sharp-eyed and even sharper-tongued sister-in-law could destroy the fragile barrier of self-protection that she was trying to erect around herself.

It was no use deluding herself, she admitted wearily now; there was no real protection, no real escape from the heartache of loving Brad. She might be able to banish him from her thoughts during the day but she had no control over her subconscious at night, and she had lost count of the number of times she had woken up, her face wet with tears, aching with loneliness and longing for him...

'Good, I'm not the last, then.'

Claire smiled as Star came hurrying towards her.

'Poppy not here yet?'

Claire shook her head as she smiled at the younger woman. 'She will be coming, though,' she told her. 'I spoke to her the other day.'

'Mmm...she may be coming, but if the gossip I've heard is true she won't—' Star broke off as Poppy herself came into the conservatory.

If the gossip was that Poppy had fallen in love with someone new, then her appearance certainly didn't bear it out, Claire reflected compassionately as she smiled at the new arrival. If anything, Poppy looked thinner and more unhappy than she had done the last time Claire had seen her.

As she patted the empty chair next to her own in a motherly fashion she studied her discreetly.

Poppy had definitely lost weight and she was very much on edge, glancing nervously over her shoulder as she sat down and lowering her voice as she greeted them, even though they were the only people in the conservatory.

'Well, I don't know about you two,' Star announced, reaching for the menu that the head waiter had left on the table, 'but *I* am hungry and fully intend to celebrate our first three marriage-free months. At least mine have been—marriage- and indeed man-free,' she added archly, looking questioningly from Claire to Poppy. 'Have you two...?'

'I don't have any plans to marry,' Claire told her hastily, mentally crossing her fingers as she acknowledged her inability to claim the true spirit of their pact.

'Nor do I,' Poppy echoed, but her face was slightly flushed and Claire could have sworn that she saw the sheen of tears in her eyes before she blinked them away.

Poor girl; was it her love for Chris that was the cause of them or was there someone else? If so...

As she made a pretence of studying the menu Claire sent up a small, heartfelt prayer that whatever unhappiness was presently clouding Poppy's life would soon be lifted and that she would enjoy the happiness and fulfilment that a girl of her age should have.

And as she made her private wish it struck Claire how much she had changed...how much knowing Brad had caused her to change. Three months ago her prayer would not have been as heartfelt simply because she would not have known what the three of them were missing...what true emotional and sexual fulfilment was.

Now that she had known fulfilment, if only fleetingly and briefly, she hated to think of the two younger women seated at the table going through their lives without knowing it.

Women, her sex, she was convinced, no matter how strong or successful they might appear in public—in the eyes of the world—had a need to focus their lives at an emotional, personal level that was so deep-seated, so intrinsically a part of their nature that it could never be totally ignored.

That, she suspected, was her sex's greatest weakness...and its great strength?

'To us—to single, unfettered emotional freedom and to celibacy,' Star toasted when they had all been served with their main course and the waiter had left.

Dutifully Claire raised her glass to join in the toast, but as the glass touched her lips she discovered that they were trembling slightly, her mind filled by an achingly clear image of Brad.

If she closed her eyes now she knew that she would almost be able to taste his mouth...his kiss...*him* on her lips in place of the suddenly too bitter sharpness of the wine. Now it was her turn to blink away unwanted, betraying, emotional tears.

Brad! If she could wipe away her memories, expunge the knowledge of how it felt to love him, of how it had felt to be physically loved by him—if she could forget for ever the sound of his voice as he'd gently coaxed her to confide in him...would she do so?

Claire was jolted back to reality as Poppy suddenly jumped up from the table, pushing back her chair, her face a sickly shade of grey-white, perspiration beading her upper lip.

'I'd better go and see if she's all right,' Claire told Star, getting up. 'You don't think she's suffering from some kind of eating disorder, do you?' she asked anxiously, conscious of how very thin the younger girl looked and the way she had been toying with her food without really eating anything.

'I don't know,' Star told her, 'but if the gossip I've heard is true it's...' She paused as the head waiter came hurrying to the table to announce that there was a telephone call for her.

'I'd better take it,' she told Claire. 'Will you excuse me?'

Nodding, Claire hurried across the conservatory. To her relief, when she walked into the cloakroom Poppy was standing in front of the mirror brushing her hair, a little more colour in her face than there had been when she had rushed away from the table.

'I'm sorry about that,' she apologised wanly to Claire. 'It must have been something I've eaten. But...er...not here...' she added hastily as Claire looked concerned. 'I—'

'Of course; you've been away on business, haven't you?' Claire remembered. 'Your mother mentioned it when I rang to check if you were going to be able to make it for lunch. A conference, wasn't it? In Italy?'

To Claire's astonishment a dark tide of colour had swept over Poppy's previously too pale skin, leaving it a bright scarlet.

Why on earth should her mentioning her business trip to Italy have provoked such a self-conscious response? Claire wondered as they both made their way back to their table, but she was too kind to draw attention to Poppy's embarrassment or to make any comment about it when Star joined them.

'So, same place, same time...same rules in three months' time?' Star said when Claire had settled the bill. 'Unless, of course, either of you have been withholding anything...?'

'Three months,' Claire confirmed, quickly getting out her diary and flicking through the pages. 'That's fine by me...' Did her voice sound as hollow to the other two as it did to her? she wondered.

Outside the restaurant, Star announced that she had an afternoon appointment with Tim. 'That was him on the phone just now. He wanted to tell me that head office are considering the outline PR plan I put forward, but it seems that I might have to fly over to America to discuss things in more detail. Not that I mind, just so long as they're paying the bills.

'You've met this Brad who heads the business, haven't you?' she asked Claire. 'What's he like?'

'He's...he's very...very pleasant,' Claire managed to stammer, and ignored the way Star's eyebrows lifted interrogatively as she waited for her to expand on her admittedly unenlightening comment.

'I...I didn't... I hardly knew him, really,' she told her bleakly, telling herself that it was, after all, the truth; the man she had thought she had known could not really have existed, otherwise he would not have walked out of her life in the way he had. The man she'd *thought* Brad was had been created by her own imagination, her own need, she told herself bitterly. *She* had created him and, in doing so, had also created her own heartache and misery.

'Mmm...well, it seems that he's now taken over the running of the company and that he intends to realign the working of the British side of things so that it runs efficiently and generates more sales; hence the new PR programme.'

Claire gave her a painful smile. It seemed that Star knew more about what was going on in Brad's life than she did, but why should that surprise her? She had purposely not mentioned Brad to Tim or Irene, not given in to the temptation to ask any questions about him and what he might be doing, but it hurt almost unbearably nonetheless to hear someone else discussing his plans...his life...his future... A future that did not, could not include her.

As Star drove off Claire turned to Poppy and was just about to ask her if she felt well enough to drive or if she would prefer a lift when a Jaguar suddenly came to an abrupt halt in front of them.

Claire heard the swift indrawn hiss of Poppy's breath as the driver got out. She almost seemed to shrink back as he strode towards her, grimly taking hold of her arm and pushing her unceremoniously in the direction of his car.

Claire watched them thoughtfully. She didn't envy Poppy her ride home with him, she decided ruefully as he slammed the door on the young woman and then walked round to the driver's side of the car.

Claire had virtually driven all the way home when, on a sudden impulse, she turned the car round and, parking at the side of the road, climbed out and walked towards the entrance to the small park where she had first seen Brad.

There weren't many children in the park today. Claire paused to watch a duck with her now half-grown babies paddling purposefully across the small pond towards her. A slight smile touched her lips as she shook her head and told her, 'Sorry, Mama Duck, but I don't have any bread.'

'I do,' a warmly rough male voice said in her ear, transfixing her with disbelieving shock. 'Or, at least, I have an airline sandwich.'

Claire couldn't move, couldn't speak...couldn't so much as look over her shoulder just in case the unthinkable had finally happened and she had begun to suffer daytime delusions that Brad was with her as well as night-time longings for him.

'Claire...speak to me...say something, please, even if it's only "Get the hell out of here"...'

All at once Claire felt her self-control snap. She started to tremble—physically violent shudders that made her whole body shake—tears blinding her as she struggled to focus on Brad's face, seeing only his blurred outline through the humiliating self-betrayal of her uncheckable tears.

'Claire, Claire, please don't,' she heard Brad groan. 'I never meant to give you such a shock. I came here on impulse to try and find the courage to call you and...Claire...'

Claire tensed as he suddenly reached for her, wrapping her fiercely in his arms, holding her so tightly that she could feel the heavy thud of his heartbeat.

The familiar, ached-for scent of him enveloped her, dizzying and deluding her senses into the belief that he wanted her, and, of course, her body reacted immediately and passionately to that belief—so much so that she was scarlet-faced with embarrassment as she felt him check slightly when he saw and, she suspected, felt the betraying thrust of her nipples against the soft silkiness of her shirt.

It was a thoroughly modest and proper shirt, buttoned well past her cleavage, with a neat, small V-neck and made of a sensible mixture of man-made fibre and natural silk—not the kind of blouse that could ever be described as either deliberately alluring or provocative—and yet suddenly, humiliatingly, she was uncomfortably aware of the way her breasts were pushing openly against it and the way...

'Oh, God, Claire, have you had any idea what you're doing to me?' she heard Brad protesting thickly, but he didn't remove his gaze from her body, and having lifted his hand to shield her body from the stare of a passer-by he didn't immediately let it drop to his side again, and Claire knew with suffocating certainty that one deep breath, one small movement was all it would take to have the warmth of his palm pressed against her and...

'Claire.'

She wasn't going to move, wouldn't have moved at all if the shock of the anguish in Brad's voice hadn't jolted her...unbalanced her.

And, of course, it was only natural that Brad should reach out to save her. And just as natural that his gaze should fix avidly and hungrily on her mouth as it half opened in a small, startled gasp when his palm moved

with quick, half-rough and totally male intensity over
the fabric-covered curve of her breast, again and again,
as though he couldn't believe that he was actually
touching her, as though his skin, his hand, his body was
greedily hungry for the physical feel of her.

This couldn't possibly be happening to her, Claire decided weakly as his other arm curved round her, binding
her to him, and his mouth finally covered hers.

She could not possibly be standing here, in her local
park, in full view of anyone who happened to be passing,
being kissed by Brad with such passionate intensity that
if he hadn't been holding her up she doubted that she
would have had the strength left in her body to stay
upright.

And, since it couldn't possibly be happening, there
was nothing to stop her throwing herself heartily into
her small, private fantasy, was there? No reason why she
shouldn't abandon all the restraints she had once thought
such an intrinsic part of her personality and respond to
Brad as she had once responded to him in the privacy
of his bedroom—as she responded to him every night
when she dreamed that she lay naked in his arms, his
body hard with longing against hers ... just the way it
felt now ...

It took the amateurish wolf-whistle of a passing
schoolboy to bring them both back to reality. Scarlet-
faced, Claire looked uncertainly into Brad's eyes as he
reluctantly released her.

'Did you walk here?' he asked gruffly. He was still
holding onto her hand and still looking at her as
though ... as though ...

Silently Claire shook her head, not trusting her voice.

'We'd better take our time driving back to your place,'
Brad told her. 'Because once we *are* there it's going to
be one hell of a long time before we do any sensible

talking... a hell of a long time before I can do anything other than make love with you. God, Claire, do you *know* how much I ache for you right now? If that damned bush over there was just a little bigger...'

Claire couldn't, even though she knew she was playing with fire, just couldn't help glancing wistfully towards the bush in question, an unremarkable rhododendron which would certainly not afford two full-grown adults enough privacy to make love.

'Claire,' Brad growled teasingly.

'I've missed you so much...' Claire's voice wobbled slightly. She swallowed hard and then admitted, 'I've wanted you so much...'

'Not half as much as I've wanted you,' Brad told her fiercely. 'If you had, you'd have returned my phone call instead of letting me think—'

'*Returned* your phone call?' Claire stared at him.

'Yes, I left a message with Tim when I couldn't get hold of you, asking you to call me.'

'I never got it,' Claire told him blankly. 'Tim just said that you'd rung. He was under an awful lot of pressure,' she defended her brother-in-law when she saw Brad's face. 'I expect it just slipped his mind. After all, *he* didn't know... he probably just thought you wanted to ask me to forward your things on or something.'

'Or something,' Brad agreed ruefully. 'When you didn't ring, I thought you were trying to tell me that you'd had second thoughts... that you didn't, after all, feel as I felt... that you didn't... There's only so much a man can do without feeling that he's pressuring a woman... harassing her. I told myself that if that was what you wanted then I owed it to you to keep out of your life, keep away from you...'

'But you are here,' Claire pointed out, holding her breath. Was he going to tell her that seeing her was accidental, that he was simply here on business...?

It wouldn't alter anything, of course—wouldn't change the fact that he obviously still wanted her. He had apparently never stopped wanting her, but her sore, tender heart yearned to know that *she* was the *cause*, the *reason* for him being here...even if she was being unrealistic and even a tiny little bit unfair...

'Mmm...' Brad agreed, his mouth quirking into a wry smile as he admitted, 'OK, maybe I'm not such a good modern new man as I like to think... Maybe I *did* think it was worth giving it one more shot, or maybe I missed you, wanted you such a hell of a lot that I just couldn't help myself,' he told her sombrely.

'Three days ago my uncle Joe told me that a man's real home, his real family...his real life lies where his heart is...with the woman his heart is with—and I knew that he was right. I came over on the first flight I could book. I've been sitting in this park for close on an hour, trying to work out what I was going to say to you and what I was going to do if you rejected me.'

'And if I didn't...if I don't reject you?' Claire asked him, hardly daring to breath. '*You* are my life now, Brad,' she continued. 'I loved John—he was strong when I needed a father-figure—but I realise now that there are different forms of love and what I feel for you—as a man, as a *lover*—is difficult for me to express here, in public. My car is parked close by,' she added breathlessly. 'We could be home in five minutes, and—'

'Oh, no,' Brad told her, catching hold of her free arm and holding onto her. 'Oh, no, ma'am, that's not the way it's going to be... Not this time; no way... This time there's no way you're going to get me into bed, not unless you promise me first that you're going to make an honest man of me.

'Have you any idea what it was like for me,' he demanded mock-indignantly, 'having to be there with my family, knowing that sexually you'd used me and then walked away from me, rejected me? How do you think I'd have felt if they'd known that? If you'd got me pregnant?' he added outrageously, his face perfectly straight whilst Claire's mouth fell open in feminine indignation at his taking over of what was surely her role.

'Not that I would have minded sharing the making of our child with you,' Brad added huskily. 'I've always wanted kids of my own... Having them around kinda gets to be a habit, you know, and I kinda miss all the little ones...'

'You told me you were going to mend your boat and sail it round the world—on your own,' Claire reminded him severely, entering into the game, her heart suddenly so light... her whole body so light that she felt almost as though she could actually physically float through the air instead of walking.

'Ah, yes. Well, I was, but that was before...'

'Before what?' Claire demanded.

'Before you seduced me, beguiled me, stole my heart and my desire for independence, made me want to spend my every waking minute and all of my sleeping ones with you,' Brad told her throatily. 'Oh, yes, most definitely all my sleeping ones...'

'I thought you didn't want to go to bed with me,' Claire said provocatively as he leaned forward and started to nibble the side of her neck. Sensations so delicious that she felt positively sure that she had lost her ability to reason filled her all the way down her body, right down to her toes, which she curled up inside her shoes

as a soft tremor of exquisite pleasure shivered tantalisingly through her—a warning...a reminder of that so
much more intense pleasure Brad had...

'I didn't say I didn't *want* to,' Brad mumbled, still
nibbling at her skin. 'I just said I wasn't going to, not
unless you had promised to marry me first.'

'Marry you...?' Claire looked at him in bemused
shock. 'You want to marry me? But...'

'No buts,' Brad told her firmly. 'I'm not having these
five children we're going to have growing up thinking
you didn't love me enough to commit yourself to me.
Besides, it would give them a bad example. I'm a firm
believer in marriage. Just ask my family—'

'*Five* children!' Claire repeated, weakly protesting.
'Brad, I'm thirty-four years old.'

'So what? These days a modern woman can put off
starting a family until she's forty if she chooses to do
so. Of course, maybe I am being a little restrictive in
just saying five,' he mused. 'There *are* twins in my family
and it's a known fact that women in their thirties are
more prone to producing twins, so who's to say...? I
do like round numbers, though, don't you? So we'd have
to go for six...'

'Six,' Claire murmured faintly, round-eyed with
disbelief.

'Six,' Brad promised, apparently misreading her expression. 'But only if you promise right here and now
that you are going to marry me... Wait a minute,' he
told her, reaching for the case he had placed on the floor
beside the bench which he had obviously been sitting on
when she had walked towards the ducks.

He opened it and produced a small pocket recorder,
switched it on and held it towards her.

'Now promise me you're going to marry me,' he instructed her. 'I want some verbal evidence to make sure
you don't go back on your word... And besides,' he

added in a very different and far more serious and emotional voice, 'I just want to hear you say it, Claire. God, you can't know how often, how much I've ached to hear you say you want me over these past damned weeks.'

'Oh, yes, I can,' Claire corrected him softly. 'Because I've wanted you in just the same way and just as much... I thought when you didn't get in touch that you were trying to tell me that you didn't want any... that it was just... that I was just... Brad,' she protested huskily as he took her back in his arms, her protest silenced by the fierce, possessive and totally male hunger of his kiss.

'*I* know why you're doing this,' she told him breathlessly when he had eventually let her go, deciding on a little light-hearted teasing of her own. 'You just want to make me want you so much that I'll agree to anything just to get you into bed...'

'Mmm...has it worked?' Brad asked her softly, giving her a wholly male and very dangerous look that made her whole body shake with excited desire.

'Er...yes...I think so,' she admitted.

'You're going to *marry* me,' Brad stressed.

'I'm going to marry you,' Claire agreed.

Several hours later, still shamelessly snuggled up next to him in bed, her body deliciously, sensuously satiated by the intensity of their lovemaking, Claire marvelled that she could ever have believed that he didn't love her.

'And you're sure that you won't mind making your home in the States?'

'My home is with you,' Claire told him huskily, meaning it. 'Of course I'll miss Sally and my friends, but Sally has Chris now and, after all, she's only going to be a plane journey away... And Felicity will come with us, of course.'

'Of course,' Brad agreed, leaning over to stroke the kitten who had come upstairs to see what they were doing.

'Mmm...I wonder if the company can *afford* to charter its own jet?' Brad mused, adding with a teasing smile, 'After all, with all these kids we're going to have, it's common sense—'

'Brad,' Claire protested, 'we don't even know if I *can* conceive yet.'

'Wanna bet?' Brad challenged her, drawing her even closer to his body as he leaned across her to whisper in her ear. 'I reckon that he or she...or even they,' he added with a wicked smile as his hand caressed the warm curve of her stomach, 'is tucked up safe and sound in here right now.'

Claire laughed and accused him teasingly of wanting to ensure that she married him, but she had a sneaking feeling that he was probably right. When they had made love earlier there had been a distinct sensation within her body—a secret female sense of somehow being so totally and primitively open to him and the intense thrust of his body within hers that she had actually felt as though her womb itself was extra responsive to him. A ridiculous and nonsensical feeling, she knew, but still...

'I'd like us to be married here,' he told her softly. 'If we wait until I take you home the family will take over and then—'

'You're not worried that they won't approve of me, are you?' Claire queried, suddenly a little apprehensive.

'No way,' Brad laughed. 'They'll approve of you all right. No, I just want to have you to myself for a little while before they swoop down on us. The way I feel about you, the way I want to be with you, is still all very new and precious to me,' he told her huskily, linking his fingers with hers and then lifting her hand to his mouth, tenderly kissing each digit before lowering his mouth to her lips.

'And to me as well,' Claire whispered back against his kiss.

They were married very quietly in a small, private church ceremony just short of a month later. Just in time to prevent too much gossip about the arrival of their eight-month baby, Claire told Brad ruefully.

Her pregnancy had been confirmed the previous morning and Brad hadn't stopped saying, 'I told you so.'

'It might not have been then,' Claire had protested, but, of course, she knew that it had, and didn't really begrudge Brad his small victory—or at least only first thing in the morning when she felt horrendously queasy.

At the end of the week they would be flying out to America—first to New York and from there to Brad's home town. Claire had slightly mixed feelings about meeting Brad's family; she felt both excited and apprehensive. Brad had telephoned them to tell them that they were married and Claire had spoken to his sisters and brothers and to his uncles, all of whom had welcome her warmly into the family.

'Just so long as we're together I don't care where we live,' she had told Brad only that morning, and had meant it.

Now a smile curled her mouth as she snuggled up against Brad's side. It was mid-morning, but they had had a late night having dinner with Sally and Chris.

'I can hear the doorbell ringing,' she told Brad sleepily.

'You stay where you are; I'll go and get it,' he told her.

Claire smiled as she watched him shrug on his robe. He had the most beautiful, sexy body... Just looking at him made her catch her breath and want to reach out and touch him. He was gone about five minutes and then she heard him coming back upstairs.

'It's for you,' he told her slightly grimly, holding a beautifully arranged bouquet of flowers with a sealed note attached to it.

'Is there something or someone I ought to know about?' he asked her semi-jealously as he handed it to her.

As she took it from him Claire frowned slightly.

'I don't think so,' she responded. 'This is a wedding bouquet. It must...' Suddenly her frown melted and she broke into warm laughter as she realised why the bouquet of flowers was so familiar. It was an exact replica of the one that Sally had had—the one she had 'dropped' as she'd 'fallen' down the stairs at the reception, the one which Claire, Poppy and Star had so misguidedly caught.

As Claire explained why she was laughing to Brad she tore open the sealed note, a rueful smile curling her mouth as she read what Sally had written.

'One down, two to go!'

Take 4 bestselling love stories FREE

Plus get a FREE surprise gift!

Special Limited-time Offer

Mail to Harlequin Reader Service®

3010 Walden Avenue
P.O. Box 1867
Buffalo, N.Y. 14240-1867

YES! Please send me 4 free Harlequin Presents® novels and my free surprise gift. Then send me 6 brand-new novels every month, which I will receive months before they appear in bookstores. Bill me at the low price of $2.90 each plus 25¢ delivery and applicable sales tax, if any*. That's the complete price and a savings of over 10% off the cover prices—quite a bargain! I understand that accepting the books and gift places me under no obligation ever to buy any books. I can always return a shipment and cancel at any time. Even if I never buy another book from Harlequin, the 4 free books and the surprise gift are mine to keep forever.

106 BPA A3UL

Name	(PLEASE PRINT)	
Address	Apt. No.	
City	State	Zip

This offer is limited to one order per household and not valid to present Harlequin Presents® subscribers. *Terms and prices are subject to change without notice. Sales tax applicable in N.Y.

UPRES-696   ©1990 Harlequin Enterprises Limited

Harlequin Romance

celebrates forty fabulous years!

Crack open the champagne and join us in celebrating Harlequin Romance's very special birthday.

Forty years of bringing you the best in romance fiction—and the best just keeps getting better!

Not only are we promising you three months of terrific books, authors and romance, but a chance to win a special hardbound 40th Anniversary collection featuring three of your favorite Harlequin Romance authors. And 150 lucky readers will receive an **autographed** collector's edition. Truly a one-of-a-kind keepsake.

Look in the back pages of any Harlequin Romance title, from April to June for more details.

Come join the party!

HARLEQUIN ⬥ PRESENTS®

Coming soon...

June 1997—Long Night's Loving (#1887)

by Anne Mather

New York Times bestselling author,
with over 60 million books in print

"Pleasure for her readers."   —*Romantic Times*

and

July 1997—A Haunting Obsession (#1893)

by Miranda Lee

one of Presents' brightest stars,
with over 10 million books sold worldwide

"Superb storytelling."   —*Romantic Times*

Top author treats from Harlequin Presents.
Make this summer the hottest ever!

TA-297

Free Gift Offer

With a Free Gift proof-of-purchase
from any Harlequin® book, you can receive
a beautiful cubic zirconia pendant.

This stunning marquise-shaped stone is a genuine cubic
zirconia—accented by an 18" gold tone necklace.
(Approximate retail value $19.95)

Send for yours today...
compliments of ◆ HARLEQUIN®

To receive your free gift, a cubic zirconia pendant, send us one original proof-of-purchase, photocopies not accepted, from the back of any Harlequin Romance®, Harlequin Presents®, Harlequin Temptation®, Harlequin Superromance®, Harlequin Intrigue®, Harlequin American Romance®, or Harlequin Historicals® title available at your favorite retail outlet, together with the Free Gift Certificate, plus a check or money order for $1.65 U.S./$2.15 CAN. (do not send cash) to cover postage and handling, payable to Harlequin Free Gift Offer. We will send you the specified gift. Allow 6 to 8 weeks for delivery. Offer good until December 31, 1997, or while quantities last. Offer valid in the U.S. and Canada only.

Free Gift Certificate

Name: _____

Address: _____

City: _____ State/Province: _____ Zip/Postal Code: _____

Mail this certificate, one proof-of-purchase and a check or money order for postage and handling to: HARLEQUIN FREE GIFT OFFER 1997. In the U.S.: 3010 Walden Avenue, P.O. Box 9071, Buffalo NY 14269-9057. In Canada: P.O. Box 604, Fort Erie, Ontario L2Z 5X3.

FREE GIFT OFFER   084-KEZ

ONE PROOF-OF-PURCHASE
To collect your fabulous FREE GIFT, a cubic zirconia pendant, you must include this original proof-of-purchase for each gift with the properly completed Free Gift Certificate.

084-KEZR